PERFECTLY YOU

SANDI LYNN

SANDI LYNN ROMANCE, LLC

PERFECTLY YOU

New York Times, USA Today & Wall Street Journal
Bestselling Author
Sandi Lynn

Perfectly You

Cover Photo by Sara Eirew
Cover Design by Shanoff Designs

Editing by BZ Hercules

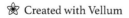 Created with Vellum

MISSION STATEMENT

Sandi Lynn Romance

*Providing readers with romance novels that will whisk them away
to another world and from the daily grind of life – one book at a time.*

BOOKS BY SANDI LYNN

If you haven't already done so, please check out my other books. Escape from reality and into the world of romance. I'll take you on a journey of love, pain, heartache and happily ever afters.

Millionaires:

The Forever Series (Forever Black, Forever You, Forever Us, Being Julia, Collin, A Forever Christmas, A Forever Family)

Love, Lust & A Millionaire (Wyatt Brothers, Book 1)

Love, Lust & Liam (Wyatt Brothers, Book 2)

Lie Next To Me (A Millionaire's Love, Book 1)

When I Lie with You (A Millionaire's Love, Book 2)

Then You Happened (Happened Series, Book 1)

Then We Happened (Happened Series, Book 2)

His Proposed Deal

A Love Called Simon

The Seduction of Alex Parker

Something About Lorelei

One Night In London

The Exception

Corporate A$$

A Beautiful Sight

The Negotiation

Defense

Playing The Millionaire

#Delete

Behind His Lies

Carter Grayson (Redemption Series, Book One)

Chase Calloway (Redemption Series, Book Two)

Jamieson Finn (Redemption Series, Book Three)

Damien Prescott (Redemption Series, Book Four)

The Interview: New York & Los Angeles Part 1

The Interview: New York & Los Angeles Part 2

Rewind

One Night In Paris

Second Chance Love:

Remembering You

She Writes Love

Love In Between (Love Series, Book 1)

The Upside of Love (Love Series, Book 2)

Sports:

Lightning

1

---

*C*harlotte
      I rolled over, opened my eyes, and stared at the empty space next to me while I ran my hand across the perfectly smooth sheet. I sighed as I sat up and grabbed my phone from the nightstand, checking to see if he messaged me back. Disappointment coursed through me and worry started to settle inside. I climbed out of bed and headed to the kitchen for a cup of coffee. As I was waiting for it to brew in my cup, my phone rang, and a smile crossed my lips when I saw it was my husband, Alex.

"Alex, I was so worried about you," I answered.

"Good morning, baby. I'm sorry. I passed out early last night. I didn't see your missed calls and text messages until this morning. Forgive me?"

"Of course. I know how tiring your business trips can be. I miss you."

"I miss you too."

"I went on a little shopping spree at Victoria's Secret yesterday."

"And I bet you bought some really sexy things. Didn't you?"

"I did." I smiled as I bit down on my bottom lip. "I was thinking we can have a Facetime date tonight and I can model something for you."

"I'd love that. I'll have to let you know when I get back to the hotel. I'm having dinner with one of the clients."

"Okay. I'll be waiting."

"I have to go, baby. I have a meeting in ten minutes. I love you."

"I love you too. Have a good day."

I ended the call, took my phone and coffee into the bathroom, and got ready for work. This was exactly how I had planned my life out: married to the love of my life, a great career, and hopefully soon, a baby would fill our happy home.

Alex and I had been married for almost seven months, but we'd been together for ten years. I met him when I was sixteen and I instantly knew he was going to be mine forever. He was the only man I'd ever been with and the only man I wanted to spend the rest of my life with.

For the past eight months, his company had been sending him to New York for two weeks at a time to meet with clients. We were both originally from California, but the day after we got married, we packed up and moved to Seattle with the company he worked for. I liked Seattle, but I missed my family, especially when he was gone two weeks out of the month, and I was left here alone. I really didn't have any friends here. Only the few that I worked with at the architect firm.

&.

I walked into the building and took the elevator up to the sixth floor.

"Good morning, Charlotte." Jessie, one of my coworkers, smiled. "A few of us are going out for drinks after work and we want you to join us."

"If it was any other night, I would. But tonight, I have a Facetime date with my husband." I grinned.

"When is he due back?" she asked as we walked to my cubicle.

"Next week." I pouted.

"You're still a newlywed. Give it a couple more years and that pout will turn into a smile when he walks out that door."

I couldn't help but laugh.

"That is one thing that will never happen to me. I love him too much."

"You'll join us next time, right?" she asked.

"Definitely." I smiled.

I sat down at my desk and turned on my computer. Before I knew it, a few hours had passed, and it was lunch time. I still hadn't heard from Alex about a time for our date tonight, so I picked up my phone and sent him a text message.

"Hi, babe. Have you figured out a time for our date tonight?"

"Hey, baby. Sorry. I've been busy. I should be back to the hotel around 9-9:30 my time. I'll call you when I get there."

"Sounds good. I'll be ready and waiting."

᠍

I changed into my sexy black nighty, ran a brush through my long brown hair, and colored my lips in red. It was six o'clock my time, which meant it was nine o'clock his time. I lay on the bed with my phone in my hand and a glass of red wine, waiting for his call. It was six forty-five and I still hadn't heard from him, so I sent him a text message.

"Are you back to the hotel yet?"

I intently stared at my phone and waited for the three dots to appear. Nothing. Another fifteen minutes passed and still nothing.

"Alex?"

Maybe his dinner ran late? This wasn't the first time he stood me up on a Facetime date. I sighed as I looked at the time and it was now eight o'clock, eleven o'clock his time. Now I was pissed. The least he could have done was sent me a text message telling me he wouldn't be able to make our date. I climbed off the bed, changed into my pajamas, and went to the kitchen for another glass of wine.

By time I got back to my bedroom, a text message from him came through.

"Sorry, baby. My phone died and dinner ran later than I thought it would. I'm exhausted, so we'll have to reschedule our date. I love you. I would call, but I can't keep my eyes open. Don't be mad, baby. I'll make it up to you."

I stared at his message as I thought about replying. There was no need. I was mad and he was going to know it. I tossed and turned all night, barely sleeping as anger was confined in my mind. A little common courtesy was all I wanted.

The next morning, I got ready for work and headed to the office. As I was walking into the building, my phone rang, and it was Alex. I let it go to voicemail because I wasn't ready to talk to him yet. Shortly after, a text message came through.

"Morning, baby. Again, I'm sorry about last night. Call me when you get a chance."

I sighed as I set my phone down on my desk. It was already hard enough when he wasn't here, and to just stand me up like that made it even harder.

"How did your Facetime date go last night?" Jessie smiled as she walked over to my cubicle.

"His dinner ran later than he thought, his phone died, and he apologized via text."

"What?" Her brows furrowed. "He didn't even call you to say he was sorry?"

"He was exhausted." I rolled my eyes.

"I'm sorry, Charlotte." She placed her hand on my arm.

"It's okay. I'm giving him the cold shoulder right now."

"Good for you. Don't let him get away with that. It's disrespectful."

"It's not the first time he's done it, and I've been really patient and forgiving. But this time, he needs to know that I'm mad."

2

Jake

"You wanted to see me, Dad?" I spoke as I walked into his office.

"Son, I need you to go to Seattle and meet with Jim Yearns. He loves our design, but he also is in love with a design from another architecture firm and he can't seem to make a decision. I need you to go there and sweep him off his feet. Make him realize that going with our firm is the better decision."

"Yeah. Sure, Dad. When do you want me to leave?"

"The day after tomorrow. I'll have Glenda book your flight and hotel for you."

"Okay. Sounds good."

"How's Christina doing?" he asked. "You haven't brought her by the house in a while."

"She's fine."

"Just fine? You've been dating for a year. Don't you think it's about time—"

"Stop, Dad." I put up my hands. "I'm in no rush."

"You're twenty-nine years old and have a great career. Next step is settling down. Your mom and I like her. We think she's good for you."

I gave him a small smile.

"Is that all? I have a lot of work to do on the Henderson project."

"Yeah, son. That's all."

I sighed as I walked out of his office. Just as I took a seat behind my desk, my phone rang and it was my best friend, Chandler.

"What's up?" I answered.

"Tell me you haven't had lunch yet. I'm in the area. How about we meet up at Umami's for a burger and a beer."

I glanced at my watch. It was one o'clock.

"Sure. I can be there in ten."

"Excellent. I'll meet you there."

I left my suitcoat on my chair and walked out of my office.

"I'm meeting Chandler for lunch. I'll be back in a couple of hours," I spoke to my secretary, Natasha. "If you need me, just call."

"Have a nice lunch, Jake." She smiled.

I climbed into my convertible BMW, put the top down, and drove to Umami's. When I arrived, Chandler was already sitting at a table waiting for me.

"What can I get you two handsome men?" The blonde-haired waitress smiled.

"I'll have the Cali burger, medium rare, and a Stella," I spoke.

"Any fries with that?" she asked.

"Sure." I smiled.

"I'll have the same," Chandler spoke.

"My dad told me today that he thinks it's time I settle down with Christina."

"And what did you say to that?"

"I told him I'm not ready, but the more I think about it, maybe it is time."

"Jake, man, don't do it. She's not the girl for you."

"I know you don't like her."

"No. I never have. I tolerate her bitch-ass because you're my best friend. But if you want the honest truth from me, I don't think you really love her."

"I love her." I furrowed my brows at him.

I wasn't sure who I was trying to convince, him or myself.

"Nah, bro. You may love her, but you're not in love with her."

"You don't know what the fuck you're talking about."

"Nobody knows you like I do, Jake, and if you marry her, you'll be making the biggest mistake of your life. You're settling because of family pressure."

"I am not."

"You are. Just last month, you told me you weren't happy. What the hell changed? Nothing. That's what."

"We went through a rough patch," I said.

"The two of you are always going through a rough patch. I'm sorry, but I cannot stand that woman."

"Watch it." I pointed at him.

He rolled his eyes and we finished our lunch. We walked out the door and as we headed to our cars, Chandler stopped me.

"Umm. Isn't that Christina over there?"

I looked over and saw her on the arm of some guy. They stopped at what I presumed was his car and shared a kiss. A kiss that lasted quite a while. My heart started racing as anger tore through me. I went to take a step and Chandler stopped me.

"Don't, Jake. Not in public. It's not worth the trouble. *She's* not worth the trouble."

I pulled out my phone and snapped a couple of pictures.

"You still want to marry her?" Chandler asked.

"I have to go. I need to get back to the office," I spoke in an abrupt tone.

I climbed into my car and sent her a text message.

"Where are you?"

"I'm getting my nails done. Why?"

"Just wondering. About tonight, I need to cancel."

"What the fuck, Jake. Why? I bought a brand new outfit and an expensive pair of shoes."

"In fact, Christina, it's over between us. I don't ever want to see you again."

"What are you talking about?"

I pulled up the pictures I took and sent them to her. It took her a minute to respond.

"I can explain. Please, let me explain."

My phone rang in my hand and it was her. I declined the call, so she called again.

"What do you want?" I shouted. "I told you it was over. I will have whatever you left at my place in a box on the porch tomorrow morning. Pick it up or else it's going in the trash. And leave your key under the mat."

"No, Jake. Please, let me explain."

"How are you going to explain kissing another man when you're in a committed relationship?" I yelled. "We're done, Christina. I don't want any explanation from you at all, because I don't even give a damn. I knew I should have broken up with you months ago."

I ended the call, blocked her number, and drove back to the office. I was pissed more than anything. Walking into my father's office, I shut the door.

"What's the matter?" he asked as he looked up from his computer.

"I just want to let you know that I broke up with Christina. We're finished."

"Jake, what happened?" he asked in a sympathetic voice.

"This is what happened!" I shoved my phone in his face.

"Shit." He sighed.

"I was at lunch with Chandler, and when we left the restaurant, she was across the street with this guy."

"Son, I'm sorry. I don't know what to say."

"You don't have to say anything because I don't want to talk about it. Do me a favor and tell Mom. I don't ever want either one of you bringing that woman's name up again."

"You don't have to worry about that. We won't. How about you join us for dinner tonight."

"No. Not tonight. I have to go. I have work to do."

I walked out of his office, and as I was passing by Natasha's desk, I told her I didn't want to be disturbed and I shut the door.

3

C harlotte

I waited all day for Alex to either call or text me asking why I hadn't called him back, but he didn't. After I left the office and was driving home, I decided it was time, so I dialed his number. He picked up on the first ring.

"Hey, baby. Are you done giving me the cold shoulder?" he asked.

"Alex, I waited for you for two hours last night."

"I know and I'm so sorry. My phone died during dinner and then the client wanted to go a bar and grab some drinks. You know I have to entertain these clients to keep their accounts. This promotion is really important to me."

"I know it is, but next time, make sure your damn phone is fully charged."

"That's my girl. I know you can't stay mad at me for too long."

"How about a date tonight?" I asked.

"I wish I could, baby, but Jeff gave me this new client that I'm meeting tomorrow morning and I have to study his portfolios so I know exactly what I'm talking about when I meet with him. You have no idea how hard this is for me. I miss you so much, it hurts."

Hearing him say that put a smile on my face.

"I miss you too."

"I promise I'm going to make this up to you. I have to run, baby. I'm swamped with paperwork. I love you."

"I love you too."

I ended the call with a sigh as I pulled up to our rental home. The reason we rented was because with the wedding and sudden transfer from Los Angeles to Seattle, we didn't have time to go house hunting. I had been looking at houses on and off while he was away, but he told me not to worry about it because we'd more than likely be moving to New York in less than a year's time.

A couple days had passed, and as I was sitting at my desk, my phone rang, and it was my sister, Jillian.

"Hey, sis," I answered.

"Hey, Charlotte. I need to talk to you."

"Okay. I'm just getting ready to go to lunch. What's up?"

I grabbed my purse from the desk drawer and locked my computer.

"God, I can't do this," she spoke.

"Jillian, what's wrong? Are you okay? Are Mom and Dad okay?"

"They're fine. Charlotte, you know how much I love you. You're my baby sister and it's my job to protect you."

"What on earth are you talking about? You're really starting to freak me out."

"I just sent you a text message."

Before I got out of my chair, I opened up the text message she sent me which contained several images of Alex and another woman. Instantly, I could feel the vomit rise in my throat as my body started to sweat and my heart pounded out of my chest. Tears filled my eyes.

"Charlotte?"

"What the fuck, Jillian!" I yelled. "What is this? Is this some kind of joke?"

"I swear to God I wish it was. I'm so sorry. I was in New York for three days at a law conference, and a few of us went out to dinner. That's where I saw him."

"Did he see you?"

"No. He didn't."

"What night was this?" I asked as the tears streamed down my face.

"A couple of nights ago. I didn't want to do this but you know how much I hate that man and you deserve so much better."

"I have to go."

I ended the call and sat at my desk. My body shook as I stared at the pictures of my husband holding hands and kissing another woman. I quickly got up out of my seat and ran to the bathroom, locking the stall door and vomiting in the toilet.

"Charlotte, are you okay?" Jessie asked as she opened the bathroom door.

"I think I'm coming down with the flu. Can you please tell Casey that I need to go home?"

"Yes, of course. Do you need me to get you anything?"

"No. I'm fine. Please just go tell him."

I wiped my mouth, stood up, and walked out of the bathroom. I was shaking so bad, I could barely make it to the elevator. As soon as the doors opened to the lobby, I walked out of the building with tears flowing from my eyes. As I reached in to grab my sunglasses from my purse, I dropped it and all the contents spilled out onto the sidewalk. That was when I really lost it. I bent down as I sobbed, trying to collect my things with shaking hands.

"Miss, are you all right?" A man knelt down next to me and started grabbing my things. "Let me help you."

I looked up into his dark brown eyes and I was humiliated.

"I've got this. But thank you." I sniffled as I wiped my eyes, noticing the mascara that was smeared on the back of my hand.

He picked up my keys and handed them to me.

"Are you okay to drive?" he asked.

"I said I'm fine. Thank you for your help."

I put on my sunglasses, stood up, and unsteadily walked to my car. My head was a mess and I couldn't think straight. Should I call him? Should I text him? Should I kill him?

"UGH!" I screamed as I gripped the steering wheel.

I entered the house and went directly to the bedroom and curled up in a fetal position on the bed while I uncontrollably sobbed. The one thing I was certain of was that I needed my family. I grabbed my phone and dialed Jillian.

"Charlotte, thank God. I'm so worried about you. Mom and I are on a plane to Seattle first thing tomorrow morning."

"Okay," I cried. "How could he do this to me, Jillian?"

"He's an asshole, Charlotte. I'm so sorry. I want you to listen to me. Whatever you do, do not text him or call him. You didn't, did you?"

"No. I can't bring myself to."

"Good. Don't. Just wait until we get there."

I managed to climb off the bed and change into a pair of sweat-pants and a tank top. I was sick to my stomach as I could feel the pain of my heart breaking in half. I went into the bathroom and looked at myself in the mirror. My face was red and my mascara-stained eyes were swollen. I cleansed my face as the tears kept streaming down. Suddenly, my phone dinged with a text message from him.

"Hey, baby. I haven't heard from you all day. How is everything going?"

I could feel the vomit rise in my throat and I ran to the toilet and hugged it. I'd never in my life felt such betrayal. My phone dinged again, and when I looked at it, there was another text message from him.

"Charlotte?"

If I didn't respond, he'd keep texting, or worse yet, he'd call. I wiped my mouth, flushed the toilet, and started typing, even though it made me sicker than I already was.

"Everything's fine. Been tied up at work on a new project. Have a meeting in five. TTYL."

"Maybe we can have our Facetime date tomorrow."

I stared at his last message before throwing my phone down on the bed. I needed a drink to numb the shattering pain I felt. As I looked around our bedroom, it was too much to handle. Everything was him. I needed to get out of here to try and clear my head, if that was even possible. I stepped into the shower and let the warm water shelter me. Once I was finished, I put on some makeup, ran a brush through my brown locks, slipped into my favorite skinny jeans and a tank top, threw on some heels, and called an Uber. I already knew it wasn't going to be safe for me to drive home.

4

Jake

I watched her as she crossed the parking lot and climbed into her car. She was beautiful and obviously broken. She was shaking from head to toe and I didn't think it was a good idea she drove in that condition, but who was I to stop her. When she looked up at me, the first thing I noticed was her beautiful sad brown eyes with the mascara stains underneath them. I looked up at the building she came out of. *Croft & Nolan Architecture Firm.* I wondered what happened that had her so upset.

I continued walking down the street until I reached the restaurant where I was meeting with Jim Yearns. I knew this account was important to my father and our company, so I needed to make sure I secured it. I still couldn't stop thinking about what a damn fool I was for staying with Christina as long as I did. Chandler was right; I didn't love her, and I damn well knew it. I just wouldn't admit it to myself. Why? Who the hell knew? Maybe I stayed because of convenience. At first, things were good. That only lasted a couple of months and then feelings of being trapped started to settle inside me. Now I was free of her and it felt so damn good.

After my lunch meeting with Jim, I headed back to my hotel and did some work. It was a beautiful day in Seattle, and instead of sitting in my room, I decided to go out and explore the city, even though I'd been here several times. I walked down the street and ended up at Pike Place Market. I looked around and picked up a beautiful hand-made bracelet for my mom with her name on it. She liked stuff like that. I grabbed some dinner and then headed to a bar to have a couple of drinks before heading back to the hotel for the night.

As I was sitting on a stool drinking my scotch, my phone rang, and Chandler was calling.

"What's up, buddy?" I answered.

"How's Seattle?"

"It's good."

"It's awful noisy. Where are you?"

"In a bar having a scotch before heading back to the hotel."

"Meet any hot chicks yet?"

I smiled because I thought about the one I met on the street, but I wasn't about to get into that with him. Plus, I didn't really meet her. I just helped her pick up her things.

"Nah."

"Dude, you're single now. Go get some pussy before you come back home."

I rolled my eyes. "I'm good, Chandler."

Suddenly, someone caught my attention out of the corner of my eye. When I glanced over, I couldn't believe it. The girl from earlier was standing at the bar a few feet away from me ordering a drink.

"Chandler, I have to go. I'll talk to you later." I ended the call and placed my phone in my pocket.

She ordered a Cosmo, and by the looks of it, she'd already had one too many, judging by the way she was stumbling and the three stamps on her hand. I watched her as she sat down on the stool, took a large gulp of her drink, and then laid her head on the bar for a few moments. I held my finger up and signaled for the bartender.

"Can I get you another?" he asked.

"No. I'm good. I don't think you should serve that girl down there anymore. It looks like she's had enough."

"I was thinking the same thing, man."

AC/DC's "You Shook Me All Night Long" came on, and suddenly, she jumped up from the stool, grabbed her drink, and hit the dance floor, twirling around while singing the words as loud as she could. I sat there and watched her. It appeared she was here alone. I'd assumed this night of drinking had something to do with whatever happened to her today.

I narrowed my eye when I saw a man approach her. I didn't like to judge people, but he looked like trouble. His fingers lightly touched the ends of her hair before making their way to her collarbone. I stood up. He lightly grabbed hold of her arm and she yanked it out of his grip, but he wasn't taking no for an answer. I walked over to the dance floor and tapped him on the shoulder. He turned around.

"She's with me," I firmly spoke.

"Nice try, buddy, but I don't think so." He turned around and tried to grab her arm again.

I stepped in between them.

"Come on, we need to get back to the hotel," I spoke as I looked at her.

"I call bullshit," the drunken man spoke. "But, being the nice guy I am, I'll let you have her all to yourself after I get done with her. It's a win/win for both of us." He shot me a disgusting smile.

"She's not going anywhere with you," I spoke as I stood tall in front of him.

"We'll see about that."

He took a swing at me and I dodged his punch. Grabbing her arm, I began to walk her to the door. She could barely stand.

Suddenly, I felt a tap on my upper back, and when I turned around, he threw a punch I didn't see coming, hitting me square in the face. I stumbled back, shook my head, and threw a punch at him as I knocked his drunk ass to the ground.

"I advise you to stay down," I spoke through gritted teeth as I pointed at him.

He lay there, unable to move, but he'd be okay. I didn't hit him that hard. I swooped the girl up in my arms and carried her out of the bar and onto the streets of Seattle. She was so out of it and she didn't know what the hell was going on. I saw a cab parked on the curb a couple of feet away and I carried her to it.

"You available?" I asked the driver.

"Yeah. Climb in."

I set her down, opened the door, and slid her inside.

"I'm not done drinking yet," she slurred.

"You are done drinking for tonight. You've had enough."

I climbed in next to her and shut the door.

"Where to?" the cab driver asked.

"Shit. Hold on a second."

Did I bring her back to my hotel to sleep it off? I looked at the small handbag she had across her body. Opening it, I pulled out her wallet and took out her driver's license. Charlotte Foster, a beautiful name for a beautiful woman. I read the address to the cab driver and had him take us there.

He pulled up in the driveway and I dug in her purse and took out her keys.

"Wait for me. I'm going to need a ride back to my hotel," I spoke to the driver.

"Yeah. Sure. It's your money," he said.

I opened the door and helped her out, trying to hold her up long enough to make it to the porch. She was practically passed out. She only had two keys on her key ring, and thankfully, I chose the right one. After opening the front door, I helped her inside and looked around.

"Come on, let's get you to bed."

I picked her up and carried her down the long hallway until I saw the master bedroom with the king-size bed. Before I set her down, she spoke, "I'm going to be sick." I carried her straight into the bathroom and leaned her over the toilet before she could vomit all over me. She dropped to her knees and hugged the bowl as I took hold of her long brown wavy hair and held it back.

"What happened to you today?" I asked in a soft voice.

She threw up multiple times in a row and the bathroom reeked of alcohol.

"Are you okay now?" I asked as she just sat there.

She slowly nodded her head as she turned and looked at me. Her eyes were red, watery, and once again, mascara stained. I reached for the wash cloth that was sitting on the counter and ran it under warm water. After wringing it out, I knelt down and wiped her mouth. She closed her eyes and passed out. Picking her up, I carried her to the bed, laid her down, and pulled off her shoes. Grabbing the blanket that was draped over the lounge chair by the window, I covered her with it. She moaned and rolled over.

I glanced over at the nightstand, saw a diamond ring lying there, and picked up the framed picture of her and her husband on their wedding day. She looked gorgeous and I wondered where the hell he was. I walked out of the bedroom, opened the front door, and looked around the porch. Going back inside, I went into the kitchen and saw a cube with some paper in it and a pen. Grabbing a piece of paper, I wrote her a note and left it by her purse on the counter.

I made sure you got home safe. Don't worry, I didn't take advantage of you. I'm not that type of guy. You needed help and I was there. Anyway, I left your house key under the white pot that's on the front porch. Take care of yourself. Take some aspirin in the morning and drink plenty of water. ~ Jake.

Before I left, I walked back into the bedroom to check on her one last time.

"I hope everything works out for you," I whispered as I stared down at her.

5

*C*harlotte
        I opened my eyes and it took a minute for them to focus. My head was pounding and my throat was so dry, I couldn't swallow.

"Oh my God," I moaned as I placed my arm over my head. "Jesus Christ, I couldn't even get into my pajamas?" I asked myself as I saw I was still fully clothed.

Struggling to sit up, I managed to throw my legs over the bed and plant my feet on the floor. I remembered absolutely nothing about last night. I didn't even know how the hell I got home. And why was I covered with this blanket? I couldn't even manage to pull the covers back? Fuck my life. I glanced over at the clock on the nightstand.

"Oh shit!"

I looked around for my phone and it wasn't near me. Stumbling from the bed, I went into the kitchen and saw my purse sitting on the counter, I grabbed it, took out my phone, and saw I had three text messages and one missed call from Alex. Fuck him. There was also a missed call and voicemail from my boss, Casey. When I dialed his number, he answered on the first ring.

"Charlotte, we were worried about you."

"I'm sorry, Casey. I'm really sick with the flu and I overslept."

"It's okay. Do you need anything? I know Alex is in New York."

"No. I'm okay. Again, I'm sorry."

"Don't be. Just get plenty of rest and get better soon. Keep me updated."

"I will. Thank you."

I set down my phone on the counter and walked over to the Keurig and started a cup of coffee. God knew I needed it badly. Opening the cabinet, I pulled out the aspirin, shook a couple pills into my hand, and chased them down with a bottle of water from the fridge. As the coffee was taking its sweet-ass time to brew, I glanced over at the island and saw a white piece of paper sitting next to my purse. I picked it up and read it.

"What the fuck?!" I placed my hand over my mouth.

Going to the front door, I opened it and lifted up the white pot, revealing my house key he left. After I grabbed it, a car pulled into the driveway and relief swept over me. Jillian got out first and ran up and hugged me tight.

"We're here for you," she spoke.

"Thanks for coming."

"Baby girl." My mom held out her arms as she stepped onto the porch.

"Hi, Mom," I spoke as the tears fell from my eyes.

"Let's go inside," she said.

"Why are you dressed like that?" Jillian asked.

"Ugh. I don't want to talk about it."

We walked into the kitchen and I took two mugs down from the cabinet and made them each a coffee.

"Umm. Who's Jake?" my sister asked. "And what the hell happened last night?"

"I couldn't be here alone, so I went to a bar or two, maybe three." I looked at my hand. "That's all I remember."

"ALONE?" Jillian shouted.

"Young lady, that was very dangerous," my mother said. "You know better than that."

"Yeah, Char, this Jake could have been a rapist or a murder."

"He wasn't. Obviously, he's a really nice guy that made sure I got home safely. Ugh. I'm so humiliated." I placed my face in my hands.

✿

*J*ake
     I was up all night thinking about Charlotte and putting ice on my face. I couldn't get the events of yesterday out of my head no matter how hard I tried. I stood in front of the mirror and stared at the bruise on my cheek. *Shit.* How was I going to explain this? I zipped my suitcase shut, and as I was leaving my hotel room, my phone rang. It was Jim Yearns.

"Good morning, Jim," I answered.

"Morning, Jake. I've got some good news for you. My company has decided to go with your firm for our new shopping mall. I was impressed with you, young man, and you better believe I'm going to let your father know it."

"Thank you, Jim. You won't regret your decision."

"I know I won't, and just so we're clear, I want you to oversee the entire project."

"Not a problem."

I climbed into the cab and headed to the airport. As I stared out the window of the plane, I couldn't help but think about Charlotte. I was worried about her, which was weird because I didn't even know her. Twice in one day, I'd helped her. What were the odds of that? I couldn't stop thinking about her wedding picture on the nightstand and her ring that was lying there. Why wasn't she wearing it and where was her husband? Better question: what was she doing bar hopping alone?

I drove straight to work from the airport. As soon as I walked into my office, Natasha was practically on my heels.

"Jake, what happened to your face?" she asked.

"Just a little disagreement with a guy in a bar."

"I hope you kicked his ass." She smiled.

"I did." I gave her a nod.

"Your dad said to send you down to his office when you got in."

"I'm on my way now. Thanks, Natasha."

I walked down to my dad's office and slowly opened the door. He took one look at my face and narrowed his eye for a moment.

"Rough trip?" His brow raised.

"It's nothing, Dad. Did Jim call you?"

"He sure did." He smiled as he got up from the chair, walked over to me, and gave me a hug. "I knew you could do it. You're the bright future of this company, son." His hands firmly planted on my shoulders. "Now, what happened to your face? Who on earth could you get into a fight with in Seattle?"

I sighed. "I was at this bar and there was this girl there who was all alone and really wasted. Some guy was hitting on her and he wouldn't stop, so I stepped in."

"That was very noble of you. I see I taught you well." He smiled. "You did kick his ass, right?"

"I took him down and made sure he stayed down and then I made sure the girl got home safely."

"That's my boy. I'm happy you're back. Why don't you come to the house for dinner tonight and bring Chandler if he's not doing anything?"

"Mom asked you to ask me, didn't she?" I cocked my head.

My dad put his hand up. "You know your mother. Since I told her about Christina, she's worried about you. Just come to dinner and make her happy. I already told her not to mention anything to you."

"Fine. I'll be there. What time?"

"Our usual seven o'clock," he replied.

"I'll call Chandler now and see if he's doing anything tonight."

❧

I had just finished changing my clothes when I heard Chandler walk through the door.

"Jake?" he shouted.

"I'll be down in second. Pour us a drink."

I grabbed my watch from the dresser and put it on my wrist as I walked down the stairs and into the living room.

"Jesus. What the hell happened in Seattle?" he asked as he stared at the large bruise on my face.

"I got into a fight with some wasted douchebag at the bar."

"Do tell." He grinned as he handed me a scotch.

"I'll get to that in a second. When I was walking to the restaurant to meet a client, there was this girl on the ground. She had dropped her handbag, and everything fell out, so I bent down and helped her. She was crying and shaking as she was trying to pick up her things. So I helped her and she went to her car. Later that night, I was sitting in a bar having a drink before heading back to the hotel for the night and she was there, alone. She was completely wasted, and some guy was trying to get her to leave with him. He was getting all handsy, so I stepped in. He didn't like that and threw a punch at me. I dodged it, grabbed the girl, and started walking her out of the bar. That's when he tapped me on the back, and when I turned around, he punched me in the face."

"Damn, bro. You better have hit him back."

"I did and I knocked him down and warned him to stay there. I picked up the girl and carried her to a cab and took her home."

"I sure hope she was worth the bruise on that pretty face of yours." He smirked.

"She's beautiful, Chandler. In fact, she's one of the most beautiful women I've ever laid eyes on."

"What did she look like?" he asked.

She's about five foot seven, petite, long brown wavy hair, and beautiful big brown eyes."

"Did you stay with her?"

"No, of course not. I got her in the house, put her to bed, wrote a note, and then left."

"Did you at least leave your phone number?"

"No. She's married." I took a sip of my drink.

"What? She was wasted at a bar alone. Where was her husband?"

"I have no clue. When I put her to bed, I saw her wedding ring lying on the nightstand and her wedding picture."

"Sounds like trouble in paradise to me. You should have left your number."

"No thanks. She's married and I don't need to get involved in that shit."

6

Charlotte

A few days had passed, and Jillian had to get back to Los Angeles, but my mom stayed in Seattle with me. As far as work was concerned, I still had the flu. My sister was a corporate attorney at one of the largest law firms in Los Angeles and she had a lot of contacts around the country. The pictures she took of Alex weren't the only ones there were. After she saw him with another woman, she got in touch with a friend of hers who was a private investigator in New York and asked him to follow him and send any pictures and reports to her. Apparently, he was staying with the woman at her apartment. That would explain why he would cancel our Facetime dates. He was spending all his evenings with her. There were pictures of them in Central Park, strolling hand in hand down the street, kissing and hugging each other. I couldn't accept it. My husband of seven months was cheating on me. The man I'd spent the last ten years of my life loving.

I was so shattered that I couldn't get myself out of bed. Jillian told me to answer his calls and respond to his text messages like normal until I figured out a plan. I wanted answers. I wanted to know why and how long it had been going on. I wanted to know why he even married me in the first place. My phone rang and it was him. My heart started racing and my mom took hold of my hand and gave it a gentle squeeze.

"It's okay, honey. Answer it," she said.

"Hey," I answered.

"Hey, baby. Feeling any better?"

"Yeah. Actually, I am."

"Good. I hate that you're sick and I'm not there to take care of you."

"Me too."

A sickness rose inside me.

"Listen, baby. I have some bad news. I have to stay another week. There's a problem with one of the accounts and they want me to try and fix it."

I swallowed hard as I slowly closed my eyes.

"Okay. I understand."

"I'm really sorry. I hate this. I hate not being there with you. I miss my wife."

I gripped the comforter with my hand so tight that my knuckles were turning white.

"It's your job and you're up for that big promotion. I understand. I'm going to be so busy anyway with having to catch up on all the work I missed."

"You're amazing. That's why I love you so much. I'm happy you're feeling better. I'll call you later to check up on you."

"Okay. Talk to you later."

I ended the call before he could say another word. Tears started streaming down my face as I looked at my mom. I now knew exactly what I had to do.

"I want to go home," I cried to her.

She reached over and placed her arms around me.

"Let's start packing."

᠙ᕀ

*T*he next morning, I stepped into Casey's office and shut the door. Nerves flooded my body as I had to admit to someone that my husband was a cheater.

"Charlotte, how are you feeling?" he asked as he stood up from his chair.

"Casey, I need to talk to you," I spoke in a saddened voice.

"Sure. Have a seat. What's going on?"

"I don't know how to say this. I'm quitting and moving back to Los Angeles."

"What?" he asked as wave of shock fell upon his face.

I took in a deep breath as tears filled my eyes.

"Alex is cheating on me with some woman in New York. I'm leaving him and I need to get out of Seattle before he gets back from his business trip."

"Gee, Charlotte, I'm sorry." He pulled out a tissue and handed it to me. "I completely understand. Am I to assume you're done here as of right now?"

"Yes. I'm so sorry that I can't give you proper notice." I dried my eyes.

"Don't worry about it. I understand. You're going to be missed around here."

He got up from his chair, walked over to me, and gave me a hug.

"I hope everything works out for you, Charlotte, and I promise you will get through this."

"Thank you. Please don't tell anyone in the office. Just tell them that I found a better job. I don't want anyone to know. I'm humiliated enough."

"I won't tell them anything. You have my word."

*W*hen I arrived home, I set the boxes I picked up down on the floor and looked up at the ceiling as tears began to spring to my eyes.

"When do you want to leave?" my mom asked as she walked over to me.

"Tomorrow morning. So let's get everything done tonight. I need to get the hell out of here."

"What are you going to do about your bank account?" she asked.

"I have my own personal account and we have a joint account where we pay the bills from. He can have it. I want nothing that reminds me of him. In fact, I'm going to run to the bank now and close my personal account down. Can you start packing my things?"

"Of course, sweetheart. Go do what you have to."

"Thanks, Mom. I don't know what I'd do without you." I gave her a hug.

When I got back home, I started taking my clothes out of the closet with the hangers still on and throwing them in the back of my car while my mom packed up all my things in the bathroom. I couldn't believe this was happening. When I stepped back into the house, my phone rang, and it was Alex. I wanted to throw it across the room, but I had a plan and I needed to act like everything was fine.

"Hello," I answered.

"Hey, baby. I haven't heard from you all day. What's up?"

"I went back to work today, and it's been crazy. I'm going to be here for a few more hours trying to catch up. Plus, Casey gave me a new project that he wants done as soon as possible."

"Oh really? I was going to Facetime you tonight for some sexy time, but I guess that's out of the question if you're working late."

Fucking liar.

"Yeah. Sorry."

"No problem, baby. We'll do it another time. I'm heading out to dinner now with a client. Enjoy the rest of your night and don't work too hard. I love you."

I took in a sharp breath and swallowed hard. I didn't want to say those words back, but I had no choice.

"I love you too." I practically choked.

I dialed Jillian and she answered on the first ring.

"Hey, sis."

"Hey. Listen, can you have your private investigator friend follow that fucker tonight. He said he was going to dinner with a client and I just want more proof."

"Sure, sweetie. I'll call him now. Mom said you guys are leaving tomorrow morning to head back here?"

"Yeah," I spoke in a somber voice.

"This is the best thing you can do. You know that, right?"

"I know. I need to be back home where I belong."

My mom and I took a break for dinner and then continued getting my things packed. When I opened the drawer of my night-stand, I saw my wedding album sitting there. Taking it out, I flipped through it, recalling how that day was the happiest day of my life. Tears started to stream down my face and then, suddenly, anger possessed me like never before. I got up from the bed and yelled for my mom.

"Charlotte, what is it?" she asked as she scurried into the bedroom.

"Start grabbing his clothes from the closet," I spoke.

"What? Why?"

"Mom, just do it."

I went to the closet, grabbed a handful of his clothes, and took them out to the firepit in the backyard. My mom followed and threw her pile on top of mine. I went back and grabbed another handful, only leaving him a couple pairs of pants and a couple of shirts. I grabbed a pack of matches from the kitchen drawer, lit one, then lit the rest and threw them on top of his clothes.

"I can't believe you just did that," my mom spoke.

"He deserves it. He deserves everything that is coming his way."

I went back inside, grabbed my wedding album, and threw it in the firepit. Then I proceeded to break some things of his things that meant the world to him.

"This is for all your lies. This is for all your deceit. This is for all the times you said you loved me."

7

*C*harlotte

I was up the entire night because the only thing I thought about was getting the hell out of this house and out of Seattle. I quickly showered, got dressed, threw my hair up in a ponytail, and grabbed my wedding ring from the nightstand so I could pawn it. Before leaving the bedroom, I took the framed wedding picture of us and threw it on the floor, stomping on it with the heel of my shoe and leaving it there for when he got home.

I drove eighteen hours straight from Seattle to my parents' house in Los Angeles. As I was driving, Jillian sent me the pictures that her friend took last night of Alex. Surprise, he wasn't at dinner with a client; he was with her. I sent him a text earlier telling him that I was super busy at work and I would be in touch with him later. He told me that he would be unavailable tonight because he was working on trying to fix that account, which I knew was total bullshit.

The moment I stepped inside my parents' house, my dad walked over and hugged me tight as I sobbed in his arms.

"Everything is going to be okay, sweetheart. I swear I'm going to kill that man."

I went upstairs and climbed into a hot bubbly bath. My heart hurt so bad that I couldn't stand it. He was the only thing I knew. I was with him for a decade and yet I was married to a total stranger. I climbed out of the tub and into bed, pulling the covers over my head and crying myself to sleep.

The next morning, as I was lying in bed, Jillian walked into the room and sat down.

"Hey." She softly smiled. "Welcome home."

"Thanks."

Suddenly, my phone rang and when I picked it up from the night-stand, an unfamiliar number appeared.

"Hello," I answered as I put it on speaker.

"Umm. Hi. Is this Charlotte Foster at 4411 Wayward Dr. Seattle?" a man on the other end asked.

"Yes. Who is this?"

"I'm sorry to bother you and I know this is going to sound strange, but my name is Jake and I was the one who helped you home that night from the bar. The one who left the note on your kitchen counter."

My eyes widened as I looked at my sister.

"Hi."

"I know this is totally awkward, so I'm just going to keep it short. I just wanted to make sure you were okay. You were pretty out of it that night."

"I'm fine. Thank you for helping me home. I'm sorry that I put you in that position."

"Please, don't apologize. It wasn't a bother at all."

"May I ask how you got my number?"

"It wasn't hard, since I had your address. I'm sorry to have bothered you and I won't call you again. I just wanted to make sure you were okay. That's all."

"Thank you. I appreciate it."

"Take care, Charlotte."

"Bye, Jake."

I ended the call as Jillian sat across from me with her mouth wide open.

"I cannot believe he found your number and called you. That's borderline stalkerish."

"I can't either. It was really nice of him. I think." I bit down on my bottom lip.

"It was nice but weird at the same time. Like I said, 'stalkerish'."

"Well, it doesn't matter. He's back in Seattle and I'm here. So if he were to stalk me at my house, I'm not there."

"True. Maybe you should block his number anyway," she said.

"I don't think that's necessary. If he calls again, then I will."

"Okay. I just wanted to stop by and check on you. I have to run. I'm meeting with a new client today."

Jake

I set my phone down and sighed. I couldn't believe I just called her. At least I knew she was okay. Great, now she probably thought I was some kind of stalker. It didn't matter. I'd never see or talk to her again. That call was a one-time thing. I hadn't stopped thinking about her since that night and I couldn't put my mind to rest until I made sure she was all right. I got up from my chair and headed to my father's office. I lightly tapped on the door before opening it.

"Jake, come in," my father spoke. "I was just getting ready to call you down. I'd like you to meet Jillian Howard. She's the new attorney who's replacing Jason."

"Nice to meet you, Jillian." I smiled as I extended my hand.

"Nice to meet you too, Jake." She returned a smile.

"Jillian is going to be working with you on the merger. She's all up to speed since Jason abruptly left."

"Great." I smiled. "Welcome aboard."

*A*s I was on my way home from the office, Chandler called.

"Hey, Chandler," I answered.

"Are you doing anything tonight?" he asked.

"I don't have plans, why?"

"Veronica is going out with the girls. You up for shooting some hoops?"

"Sure. Come over for dinner. I'll stop by the market and pick up a couple of steaks."

"Yes! You. Are. The. Man. I'll be over around seven."

"See you then." I chuckled.

I made a detour and stopped at Trader Joe's. The moment I walked in with my aviators on and my dark gray suit, heads turned and looked at me. The heads of women of all ages. I didn't have a problem attracting women. I basically could have any woman I set my sights on, and that usually got me into trouble. This past year with Christina was exhausting and also a lesson learned.

I grabbed a small shopping cart and headed to the produce section to grab some items for a salad. While I was looking at the lettuce, I glanced over and saw Jillian standing by the bakery. I grabbed a head of lettuce and walked over to her.

"Hey." I smiled. "Fancy seeing you here."

"Hey, Jake." She grinned.

The woman behind the counter asked her what she could get her.

"I'm going to take one of those key lime pies," she spoke.

"Excellent choice." I grinned.

"I'm heading over to my parents' house for dinner and key lime pie is my sister's favorite dessert ever."

"It's mine too. I'll take one as well," I spoke to the woman. "Your sister has great taste in desserts."

"I'm hoping it'll make her feel a little better."

"Why? Is she sick?"

"Sick with a broken heart. She just found out that her husband is cheating on her."

"I'm sorry to hear that. I can relate. I just broke up with my ex-girl-friend because I caught her cheating on me."

"Gee, I'm sorry."

"Thanks. But don't be. It was for the best anyway. How long has your sister been married?"

"Seven months, but they had been together for ten years."

"Jesus. That's too bad. The guy sounds like a real jerk."

"He is. I never liked him and neither did my parents. My sister is such a wonderful person and she didn't deserve this."

The lady behind the counter reached over and we both took the boxes with the key lime pies from her.

"It was good seeing you, Jillian. I hope the pie helps your sister feel a little better."

"Thanks, Jake. I'll see you tomorrow."

I gave her a smile as I pushed my cart to the meat counter. When I got home, I set the bags on the island and walked out to the patio and started the grill.

"Knock knock." I heard Chandler's voice. "I brought us some beer." He smiled.

"Thanks."

"What's wrong?" he asked as he narrowed his eye at me.

"Nothing. Why?"

"You have that look. I've known you my whole life, Jake. Something is bothering you. Spill it."

"I called her today," I said as I took down a bowl for the salad.

"Called who?"

"Charlotte."

"The married woman from Seattle?"

"Yep."

I took a knife from the drawer and handed it to Chandler. "Cut up these cucumbers for me."

"Why did you call her?"

"I just needed to make sure she was okay."

"Dude, seriously. How did you get her number?"

"The internet. I already had her address, so it wasn't hard."

"And there you have it, folks. My best friend is officially a stalker."

"I am not." I rolled my eyes.

"And you're going to tell me that she wasn't weirded out by your phone call?"

"If she was, she didn't sound like it. She thanked me and I told her that I'd never call her again and I just wanted to make sure she was all right. It's done and over with. She's fine and now she's out of my head."

He stood there as he cut the cucumbers and narrowed his eye at me.

"What?" I asked.

"I don't think she is."

"I swear she is. She lives in Seattle and she's married. End of discussion."

"Yeah, time to move on. What about that hottie that lives five houses down?"

"The stripper?" My brow arched.

"I bet she's really flexible." A smirk crossed his lips.

I sighed. "No. I'm on a dating hiatus. I'm focusing on me and me alone. It's going to take me a long time to be able to trust a woman again."

8

*C*harlotte

    I spent the day in bed looking for apartments online. As much as I loved my parents, I needed my own place. Money wasn't an issue for now, but I would have to find a job. Plus, I had attorney fees that I would need to pay. Every time my phone would ding with a text message from Alex, the anger inside me intensified.

    "Hey, baby. Haven't heard from you all day, again. You haven't forgotten about your husband, have you? Because you're starting to break my heart."

    I took in a deep breath as I read his message. I couldn't do this anymore. I couldn't keep silent. I wanted that son of a bitch to know that I knew what he was doing.

    "I'm calling you in five seconds and you better fucking pick up the goddamn phone."

    I counted to five and then dialed his number.

    "What the hell was all that about, Charlotte?" he answered in an abrupt tone. "I really can't talk right now."

    "You can't talk?" I yelled. "Why? Are you in the middle of fucking that blonde-haired whore you're with?" I screamed.

My mom and Jillian came running into my room as I put the call on speaker.

"What the fuck are you talking about? Have you lost your mind?"

"Yeah. I've lost my mind, asshole."

I clicked on the pictures that Jillian sent to my phone and sent them to him. There was a long pause.

"Where did you get these?" he asked.

"It doesn't matter. How could you do this to us? To me?"

"Baby, I swear to you. She means absolutely nothing to me. I was lonely and missing you so much and she was here. Please forgive me. We'll talk about this the second I get home. In fact, I'm getting on a plane tonight. Baby, we can work this out. I made a mistake and I feel horrible. Please."

I inhaled a deep breath as my heart pounded out of my chest.

"Baby? Everyone makes mistakes. I've been under so much pressure lately. I love you so much and I can't live without you. I'm coming home to you, Charlotte."

I swallowed hard and put on my calm sweet voice.

"You're really going to get on a plane tonight and come home?"

"Yes. I'm on the site now and the next plane leaves in two hours. I just bought the ticket. I'm coming home to you, baby. We'll work this out. I love you so much. I made a mistake and I'm so sorry."

I looked at my mom and my sister as they stood there with their arms folded, shaking their heads at me.

"Okay. I'll be waiting for you and you're going to tell everything."

"Thank God." He sighed. "I'll see you in a few hours, baby. I promise, I'm going to make things right."

"I'll see you when you get home."

I ended the call as a small smile crossed my lips.

"What I wouldn't give to be at that house when he comes home and sees that you're gone and so are his clothes." Jillian busted into laughter.

"I know." I laughed with her. But soon enough, my laughter turned into a hysterical cry.

Two Weeks Later

 he last piece of furniture was finally delivered and put in place. The past couple of weeks had been so busy with moving and meeting with my lawyer that I didn't have time to think about anything else. Needless to say, Alex was pissed as hell when he went home that night and found me gone and his clothes burnt to ashes outside in the firepit. His mother, whom I never really cared for, called me daily and asked me how I could do that to her son and that obviously I was to blame for his extra-marital activities. I told her to go to hell and then blocked her number.

I took the pink-covered journal that was sitting on the coffee table over to the couch and sat down. I'd had this journal since I was eight years old. It was my perfect life planned out. I wrote about being a straight A student in school, graduating as a valedictorian, and giving the best motivational speech of my life. Then I'd go off to college to study architecture, graduating with honors and a 4.0 GPA. I'd meet the man of my dreams and he'd sweep me off my feet. We'd get married, live in a beautiful home that I designed, have two children that we'd spoil, and live happily ever after for the rest of our lives. I'd written how much my husband loved me and only me. How I was his world, his mere existence, and how he'd never hurt me. Our souls would become one, never to be ripped apart.

As I was reading and tears were streaming down my face, there was a knock on my door.

"Charlotte, it's me," Jillian spoke.

I got up from the couch with my journal in my hand and opened the door.

"Hey." I gave a small smile as I wiped my eyes.

"Charlotte." She pouted. "Are you okay?"

"How can I be okay when the man I thought I knew turned out to be someone I never really knew at all?"

She stepped inside and hooked her arm around me.

"Go sit down and I'll grab the wine. Is this your journal?" She took it from my hand.

My sister was the only one who ever knew about my journal. I'd kept it hidden for years, and to this day, nobody else knew about it. Not even asshole Alex. She grabbed a bottle of wine and two glasses. Bringing them over to the couch, she poured our drinks and handed me a glass.

"I love you, and don't hate me for what I'm about to say. I think deep down, you knew Alex wasn't the love of your life, but you got so caught up in this perfect life you wanted so badly, that you took the first guy who looked your way."

"That is not true."

"Yes, it is. You stood by that asshole even when he treated you poorly. He's a narcissist and a manipulator. I've been telling you that for years. Everything that didn't go his way was your fault and you believed it. You wanted so badly to believe he was the one because you were afraid you wouldn't get your perfect life on *your* timeline."

"You're wrong!" I shouted.

"Am I? Am I really?"

"He did love me, Jillian."

"I'm not saying he didn't love you. But he also knew what a pushover you were. The man wanted his cake and he wanted to eat it too. If I hadn't seen him in New York, there's no telling how long this would have gone on for. And not to mention how many others there were before her."

"What the fuck!" I stood up and spewed. "How the hell could you say that to me?"

"I'm not trying to hurt you. I'm trying to make you see that the life you had with him was never perfect like you thought it was. You were blind to the shit he did and the mean things he'd say to you. Marrying him was the final notch for your perfect life and that's all you could see. Mom and Dad both knew it too. You always talked about your perfect life timeline. You settled and I don't believe you were ever truly as happy as you deserved to be."

Everything she said hit me hard. I sighed as I sat back down on the couch next to her and laid my head on her shoulder.

"What do I do now?" I asked as a tear fell down my cheek.

"You start living life. Start over. Reinvent yourself. Become Charlotte Foster without the asshole Alex in her life."

"I don't know how."

"Yes you do." She kissed the top of my head. "The first thing you're going to do is stop planning your life out. Take it one day at a time. You are a brilliant architect."

"Yeah, with no job."

"You'll find one as soon as you start looking."

"I really wish Adler Grant didn't move out of state," I said.

"I know. They were a really good firm. I'm sure they'd take you back if you wanted to move to Chicago."

"Nah. I'm good here at home in L.A. where I belong."

I did an internship back in college for Adler Grant, and the day I graduated, they hired me full-time. Three months before I was about to get married, they moved their offices to Chicago and offered me to relocate. But I couldn't and they knew it. Once I found out Alex was getting relocated to Seattle, I started looking for a job there, and the day after we got back from our honeymoon, I started at Croft & Nolan.

9

*J*ake

"How is your sister doing?" I asked Jillian.

"She's doing okay. She's settled in her new apartment now and taking things one day at a time. She hired a lawyer and started the divorce proceedings."

"Good. May I ask how she found out he was cheating?" I asked.

"Me." She pursed her lips.

"You?"

"I was in New York at a lawyer conference and he was there on a business trip at the same time. I went to dinner with some of the people from the conference and saw him with the woman at the restaurant. I took some pictures and sent them to her. I hated doing it and I had to think long and hard about it first. But I always hated that man and my sister didn't deserve to be with a scumbag like him. She needed to see what the hell he was doing all the times he made excuses as to why he couldn't Facetime or call her. Anyway, I have a friend in New York who's a private investigator and I had him follow the two of them for a few days after and report back to me."

"Your sister is very lucky to have a sister like you." I smiled.

"Yeah. That's what my husband said too. He wants to rip the guy's throat out."

"To be honest, I kind of do too and I don't even know your sister."

She gave me a small smile.

"Why would anyone ever cheat on you?" she asked. "You're such a nice guy."

"Christina was a gem. One of the rough cut ones." I smirked. "I don't think there's a guy in this world that will ever make her happy and I don't think she'll ever make any guy happy. My dad always talks about how it's time to settle down. According to him, I have my career under my belt and the next step is finding someone to share my life with. But I'm not ready for any of that. I like being single and doing my own thing."

As we continued our conversation, my father walked in.

"Hi, Jillian. Good to see you."

"Good morning, Mr. Collins." She politely smiled.

"Jake, Joe just quit."

"What? Why?" I furrowed my brows.

"Seems he's moving to Chicago. His wife's mother is very ill and she wants to be closer to her."

"That's too bad. What about his projects?"

"That's why I'm here. You're going to have to oversee them until we hire someone. I have H.R. working on an ad now."

"Dad, I really don't have time to take on any additional responsibilities."

"I know, son, but it's only temporary."

"Mr. Collins," Jillian interrupted, "Are you looking for another architect?"

"Yeah. You know someone good?"

"Actually, my sister is an architect. Graduated at the top of her class at USC."

"She's not working?" my father asked.

"She's in between jobs right now."

"Send her over with a resume and portfolio and Jake and I will take a look."

"Great. I'll tell her."

Suddenly, her phone rang.

"Excuse me. It's Greg. I have to take this." She got up and walked out of my office.

A few moments later, she popped her head in.

"I'm sorry, Jake. I have to go. One of my other clients is in a crisis."

"Sure, okay. Enjoy the rest of your day."

"Thanks. You too. By the way, when do you want my sister to come in?"

"I'm open tomorrow at eleven o'clock," I said as I checked my calendar. "Dad, will that work for you?"

"I have a meeting at ten, but I'll pop in after."

"I'll let her know. Thanks, guys." Jillian smiled.

"Wow, what perfect timing," my dad spoke. "Hopefully she's as good as Jillian says she is."

❧

*C*harlotte
  I had just walked through the door from meeting with my lawyer when my phone rang, and Jillian was calling.

"Hey, sis."

"Char, I have amazing news for you."

"What is it?"

"You have a job interview tomorrow at JAC Designs at eleven o'clock."

"What? How?"

"They're one of my clients. I was there earlier and one of their architects is moving to Chicago and they need to find someone as soon as possible. I told them about you, and they want you to come in tomorrow with your resume and portfolio."

"Jillian, I appreciate it, but I don't know if I'm ready to go back to work yet."

"Char, what did we talk about? It's time to rewrite your life and it's time to start living again. This job popped up out of nowhere. It's a sign. You better go. I'll text you the address when we hang up. Tomorrow morning at eleven o'clock."

"Okay." I sighed. "Thank you, sis."

"You're welcome. I have to go. We'll chat later."

Later that night, I was sitting on the couch looking through my calls so I could add my lawyer, Liam, to my contacts; something I should had already done but didn't. That was when I ran across the phone number from the man named Jake who made sure I got home safely from the bar back in Seattle. He had held true to his word and never called me again after that day. I didn't know what came over me. Maybe it was because I was feeling down and lonely, but I decided to send him a text message.

"Hi, it's me Charlotte. The girl you helped home from the bar. I just wanted to thank you again for what you did for me. The person you saw that night is not who I really am. That just happened to be the worst day of my entire life and I guess I needed to forget about it for one night. I just wanted you to know that for some strange reason."

I hit send and immediately thought to myself, *oh shit, what the hell did I just do?*

"Hi, Charlotte. Don't worry. I didn't judge you at all. I hope you're doing better now."

"I'm getting there. One day at a time."

"Good. I'm happy to hear that. One day at a time is the best way to go. Whatever happened, I'm sorry. I'm glad I was at the bar that night."

"Me too. Thank you, Jake. Enjoy the rest of your evening."

"You too, Charlotte. If you ever feel like talking to someone, give me a call."

*J*ake
    I couldn't believe she texted me. Damn it. She sounded down and I wanted so badly to ask her what happened, but it was none of my business. If she wanted to tell me, she would have. I smiled as I added her to my contact list. Maybe

taking another trip to Seattle wouldn't be a bad idea. Maybe we could meet up for coffee or drinks. Maybe I was just being delusional. After all, she was married, but I got the feeling she wasn't happy. I'd wait a few days and then text her again and tell her that I was going to be in Seattle. With any luck, she'd want to meet up and thank me in person. I didn't know what it was about her that made my head spin. The only times I'd seen her was when she was crying her eyes out and completely drunk off her ass. The moment she looked up at me with those beautiful brown teary eyes on the street, I was mesmerized. I sighed as I set my phone down and finished off my drink.

---

10

*C*harlotte

I was up all night thinking about the interview I was going on today. Jillian was right. It was time I started rewriting my life and reinventing myself. I loved being an architect and I was damn good at it. I'd lost myself all those years I was with Alex. The only thing I focused on was him and making him happy. And while I failed at doing that, he was being happy with someone else. How could I be so blind?

Our divorce was going to be simple, according to my lawyer. We didn't have any assets because we rented the house in Seattle. We had separate bank accounts and the joint one we did have was for bills only. Thank God I was smart enough to keep my finances separate. I learned that from Jillian. That was the way she and Chris did things. All I wanted was for this to be over with. The worst part was that I'd have to see him in court here in Los Angeles. I never wanted to see him again. My mom told me that time would heal my heart and wounds, and I was so sick of hearing that. I gave ten years of my life to that man and he hurt me in the worst possible way. I wasn't so sure I'd ever heal from what he did.

I made a cup of coffee, took a shower, threw some curls at the end of my hair, and dressed in a black tailored-fit pant suit. Just as I was slipping into my black heels, my phone rang, and Jillian was calling.

"Hello."

"Hey. You're still going, right?"

"Yes. I'm just heading out the door now," I spoke as I grabbed my portfolio and keys off the table.

"Good. I'm on my way to a meeting over that way."

"You didn't tell them anything personal about me, did you?"

"Of course not. I just sang your professional praises. Good luck and call me when you leave there. Maybe we can meet up for lunch."

"Will do. Talk to you soon."

I arrived at the building where JAC Designs was located, took in a deep breath, and walked inside with my head held high, even though I was a nervous wreck. What if they could see what a mess I was? What if they looked at me and saw nothing but a disaster?

"Welcome to JAC Designs. How may I help you?" a young man with spikey blonde hair asked.

"I have an eleven o'clock interview for the architect position." I smiled.

"Excellent. Have a seat and Mr. Collins' secretary, Natasha, will be right with you."

I took a seat in the eggplant-colored chair, crossed one leg over the other, and nervously tapped my foot on the floor.

"Hi, I'm Natasha." A fiery redhead with bright green eyes smiled as she extended her hand.

I stood up and gently shook it.

"Hi, I'm Charlotte Foster."

"Nice to meet you, Charlotte. Follow me and I'll take you to Mr. Collins' office. You'll be meeting with Mr. Collins Sr. first since Jr. is still tied up in a meeting."

"There's two of them?" I asked.

"Yes. Father and son." She smiled. "Excuse me, Mr. Collins, Charlotte Foster is here for her interview."

"Charlotte, come in." He smiled as he walked over to me and lightly shook my hand. "Thank you, Natasha."

"You're welcome. I'll send Mr. Collins in as soon as his meeting is over."

*

*J*ake
          As I sat in the conference room, I looked at my watch. It was eleven thirty.

"We need to wrap this up, people. I'm late for an interview."

I concluded the meeting and walked to my office with my file folders in hand.

"Your interview is here. She's in with your father, Jake. He said to come right down after your meeting."

"I'm on my way now." I sighed.

If there was one thing I hated, it was being late for something, but there was a problem with one of the projects and it needed my immediate attention. I walked down to my father's office and lightly tapped on the door before opening it. When I stepped inside, I stopped dead in my tracks when the woman sitting in the chair across from my father's desk turned her head and looked at me. Our eyes met and my heart started racing. She narrowed her eye at me for a moment and got up from her chair.

"I know you," she spoke. "You're the man who helped me on the street in Seattle when I dropped my purse."

"Hello, Charlotte." I smiled as I walked over to her and extended my hand. "I'm Jake Collins."

She cocked her head as a look of confusion swept over her beautiful face.

"No." She slowly shook her head. "You're not—"

"I am," I interrupted. "The same Jake that took you home that night from the bar. I'm sorry, but I'm in total shock right now that you're standing here."

"You and me both." She placed her hand in mine and gently shook it.

"You're Jillian's sister?"

"Yeah." She smiled. "So wait a minute, you're the one who helped me with my things on the street and the same man who made sure I got home safely that same night?"

"Yeah. I was in Seattle on business. I was on my way to meet a prospective client when I saw you the first time."

"Oh my God." She placed her hand on her forehead. "This is unbelievable, not to mention extremely humiliating."

"Please. Don't be humiliated. Where's my father?"

"He had to step out for a moment to take a phone call."

She sat back down in her seat and I took the seat behind my father's desk.

"Is this your portfolio?" I asked as I picked it up.

"Yes."

I thumbed through her designs. Each one was equally amazing.

"You're very talented." I smiled.

"Thank you." The corners of her mouth shyly curved upwards.

I picked up her resume and glanced at it. I couldn't believe she was here, and I was astounded that she was Jillian's sister. It all made sense now. That day, that night, why she wasn't wearing her wedding ring. She must have just found out that her husband was cheating on her.

"Congratulations, Charlotte Foster. You're hired." I grinned.

"Really? Even after what you witnessed back in Seattle?"

"You told me yourself last night over text message that you weren't that person and I believe you. From what I can see, you're extremely talented."

"Don't you want to know why I left Seattle after such a short period of time?"

"You'll tell me when you're ready."

The door opened and my father walked in.

"Oh good. The two of you met. I'm sorry, Charlotte, but I had to take that."

"It's fine, Mr. Collins. I understand."

"I was just congratulating Charlotte on becoming a new employee here at JAC Designs," I said.

"Good. From what I saw, I think she'll be an excellent asset to our company. Can you by chance start tomorrow?" my father asked her. "We're in a pinch and have a few deadlines looming over us."

"Yes, of course."

"Excellent. It was a pleasure meeting you, Charlotte." My father extended his hand.

"The pleasure was all mine, Mr. Collins." She smiled as she lightly shook it. "Thank you both for this opportunity. I promise I won't let you down."

I gave her a small smile as she walked out of the office and shut the door.

11

Charlotte

I walked out of the building as my heart raced at the speed of light and the humiliation that Jake, who was now my boss, was the guy from Seattle. The guy who saw me having a breakdown on the sidewalk, and the same guy who saw me drunk off my ass and probably acting like a complete fool at the bar. Oh my God, this was nothing short of a nightmare.

I pulled out my phone and sent a text message to Jillian. I was furious at her for not telling me about him.

"We need to meet for lunch now!!!!! Jon & Vinny's. I can be there in fifteen."

"I'm not sure I'm liking all those exclamation points. Did the interview go okay?"

"FIFTEEN!!!!"

"Okay, okay. I'll be there."

I arrived first and took a seat in a booth where I sat facing the door, waiting for my sister to arrive.

"Hi there. I'm Lily and I'll be taking care of you. Are you waiting for someone?" she asked.

"Yes. My sister."

"Great. Can I get you something to drink while you wait?"

"Two glasses of Pinot, please."

"Of course." She smiled.

I rested my elbow on the table and placed the palm of my hand against my forehead. Suddenly, my phone dinged. Pulling it from my purse, I saw I had a text message from Jake.

"It was good to see you again, Charlotte," he wrote and attached the smiley emoji at the end.

Oh my God. I didn't know how to respond.

"Thanks. See you tomorrow morning."

Lily walked over and set the glasses of Pinot down. One glass in front of me and the other across from me where Jillian would be sitting. I reached for it and looked at her.

"Both glasses are for me."

"Oh. I'm sorry."

Jillian walked into the restaurant and slid in across from me.

"Oh, you ordered me wine. Thanks." She smiled as she reached for my glass.

I smacked her hand away.

"They're both mine!" I snapped.

Lily walked back over, and Charlotte ordered herself a glass of wine. We quickly placed our lunch order since we both already knew what we wanted.

"Jesus, Charlotte. What the hell happened at that interview? Didn't it go well?"

I gulped down the first glass as I stared at her.

"The man who interviewed me, Jake?"

"Yeah? He's so hot and super sweet." She smiled.

"Does the name ring a bell to you?" I swirled my finger at her.

"No. Should it?"

"Jake. Jake. Jake. Think about it, Jill!"

I picked up my second glass and took a sip. She sat there narrowing her eye at me for a moment and then it suddenly hit her. Her eyes grew wide as she placed her hand over her mouth.

"No. He's not—"

"Oh, but he is, dear sister. And what you don't know is that right after you called me and sent me those pictures of Alex, I flew out of the building and dropped my purse and everything fell out all over the sidewalk. He just happened to be walking by, saw me in a total oblivious mess, and knelt down next to me and helped me pick it all up as I sat there shaking and crying my eyes out."

"Wait a minute. He helped you during the day and at the bar that same night?"

"Yep." I took a drink of my wine. "He was on business in Seattle meeting with a potential client."

"Oh shit." She threw her head back.

"What? What was that for? Why the 'oh shit'?"

"We've been working together a lot and, you know, we talk." She suddenly got quiet.

"Talk about what?" I cocked my head.

"I may have told him about your situation."

"Oh my God!" I yelled and everyone in the restaurant turned their heads. "You told him about Alex?" I leaned across the table.

"I didn't use your name and I didn't know he was 'the Jake.' Do you know how many Jakes there are in the world? What are the chances?"

"I texted him last night!!" I exclaimed as I finished off my second glass of wine.

"What? Why the hell would you do that?" she asked.

"I don't know. I was looking for my lawyer's number to add him in my contacts and I ran across his. I just wanted to thank him again, and now he's my boss and he knows the gory details of my life."

"Yay!" She smiled brightly. "You got the job?"

"Yes." I sighed as I placed my hand on my forehead.

"That's awesome, Char. I knew you would. You're going to love working there. They are some of the nicest people I have ever met."

"Do you not realize how humiliated I am?"

"Listen." She reached over and placed her hands on mine. "You had every right to act the way you did that day. He knows your situation and he's not going to judge you for that. He's dangerously hot, isn't he?" She grinned. "Come on, admit it."

"Yeah. He is. But still.."

Lily brought us our food and asked if I wanted another glass of wine.

"No. Thanks. I'll just have a glass of water."

"Coming right up," she said.

"He was just in a relationship for about a year," Jillian said as she stabbed her fork into her salad.

"Was?" I asked.

"Yeah. He caught her cheating on him."

"Oh. I know the feeling."

"Don't tell him I told you. So see, he can relate to your bad day."

"I wonder what he did to make her cheat?"

"Really?" Jillian's brow raised. "Did you do anything to make Alex cheat? No. You didn't. Some people are just assholes and don't know a good thing when they have it," she said as she pointed her fork at me.

12

Jake

"She's a nice girl and very talented," my father spoke. "Maybe you should have checked her references first before you went and hired her." His brow raised.

"She needs the job, Dad, and obviously, she's very qualified."

"She's young."

"She's twenty-six. Three years younger than me."

"She was only at her previous job for about seven months," he said.

"She had to move back to Los Angeles. She had no choice."

"What's going on, son?" he asked as he narrowed his eye at me. "I feel like there's something you're not telling me."

I inhaled a sharp breath.

"She's the woman I took home that night from the bar in Seattle."

"You're kidding."

"No. I'm not. She's also the woman I helped on the sidewalk earlier that day. I was on my way to meet Jim at the restaurant when I saw her on the sidewalk. She was distraught and she dropped her purse and everything fell out."

"What happened to her?"

"She found out that her husband of seven months was cheating on her."

"Oh." He leaned back in his chair.

"Jillian told me everything without knowing that I was the one who made sure her sister got home safely. She moved back here because this is where she grew up and her family is here. She's divorcing her husband. They had been together since she was sixteen."

"Gee. Poor girl. Okay, that makes sense now."

"Please don't tell her that I told you any of this. She was already humiliated enough when I walked into the office and she saw me."

"I won't. It sounds like JAC Designs will be a fresh start for her."

"I think it will be. I have work to do," I said as I headed towards the door.

"Okay, son. I'll talk to you later."

I sat at my desk, leaned back in my chair, placed my hands behind my head, and thought about Charlotte. She looked so beautiful and I couldn't believe she was here and now working for us. I felt bad for Jillian's sister as it was, but now I felt even worse knowing it was Charlotte that it happened to.

My office door opened, and Jillian stood there and stared at me.

"Jillian? Come in."

"I had no idea you were 'the Jake' that helped my sister that night. Just like I had no idea you were the one who called her on the phone."

"You know about that?" I asked.

"I was there. That was the morning right before I came here for the first time. Thank you for looking after her at the bar. What exactly happened that night?"

"I was sitting at the bar having a drink and she walked up and ordered another one for herself. She was really wasted as it was, and I told the bartender he needed to cut her off. Then a song came on and she ran to the dance floor and started dancing. Some guy walked up to her and was trying to get her to leave with him. So I stepped in and we had a bit of an altercation."

"Oh my God. Did he hit you?"

"Yeah." I smiled. "But one punch from me and he went down. I picked your sister up, carried her out of the bar, and I put her in a cab. When I finally got her into the house, she told me she was going to be sick, so I took her to the bathroom and held her hair back while she vomited. When she was done, she pretty much passed out. So I laid her on the bed, wrote her a note, and left."

Tears filled her eyes.

"Thank you. Something serious could have happened to her if you weren't there. Does she know about the guy and the vomiting part?"

"No." I lightly laughed. "I don't think so."

"Well, don't tell her. She's already freaking out as it is."

"Why?"

"Because she's afraid of what you think of her."

"I already told her that I didn't judge her and not to be embarrassed."

"Yeah, but she's Charlotte and she cares what people think; a little too much sometimes. Thanks for hiring her. She's really good at her job. I promise you that you won't regret it."

"I could see that from her portfolio, and I know I won't regret it. She more than qualified."

"This is going to be a new start for her." She lightly smiled.

"Well, I'm glad I could help with that."

&.

*C*harlotte
　　　　Later that night, I went over to my parents' house for dinner. Jillian and Chris pulled up at the same time I did.

"Hey, Charlotte." Chris kissed my cheek. "I heard about your new job. Congrats."

"Thanks, Chris."

We walked into the house and while Chris met my father in the living room, Jillian and I went to the kitchen.

"There's my girls." My mom smiled. "Jillian, you can make the salad, and Charlotte, you can start mashing the potatoes."

"Guess what, Mom?" I said.

"What?"

"I got a job today."

"You did? That's wonderful. Where?"

"JAC Designs."

"Aren't they a client of Jillian's?" she asked.

"Yes. She's the one who told me they were hiring. I had an interview this morning and they hired me right on the spot."

"I'm so happy for you, Charlotte. See, everything is moving along in the right direction."

"Guess who her boss is?" Jillian chimed in.

I looked at her with my evil sister look and she just smiled at me.

"Who?" My mom looked at me.

"Jake Collins," Jillian said.

"Do I know him? The name doesn't sound familiar."

"He's the Jake who made sure she got home safe from the bar in Seattle. You know, the one that left the note on the kitchen counter."

"What? How is that possible? I thought the man that helped you lived in Seattle."

"So did we," Jillian said. "Turns out, he was just on business there and happened to be at the right place at the right time."

"Well, I want to meet that man and thank him for what he did. I'm going to have him over for dinner one night."

"Oh no you're not," I said. "He's my boss and we're going to forget all about that night. Understand me?"

"But, Char—"

"No buts!" I held up the masher.

I heard my phone ringing in my purse, and when I pulled it out, I saw it was my lawyer calling.

"Hello," I answered. "Are you serious? Damn him. I hope you told him that it'll be a cold day in hell before that happens. Okay. Thanks for calling and letting me know."

"What was that about?" Jillian asked.

"It seems as though Alex is suing me."

"Suing you for what?" She laughed.

"He's suing me for all of his clothes I burned and the things I broke. Apparently, I caused him a great deal of mental stress and he's seeking damages in the sum of fifty thousand dollars."

"Oh my God." Jillian laughed. "What did your lawyer say?"

"He said that we're going to go after him for my own emotional damage and distress, and that he'll let me know when the court date is."

"Oh baby." My mother hugged me. "Don't worry. He's not going to get a dime."

"I'm on this," Jillian said as she grabbed her phone and walked out of the kitchen.

13

Charlotte

I swallowed hard and took in a deep breath as I approached Jake's office. After lightly tapping on the door, I heard him tell me to come in.

"Charlotte." He smiled. "Good morning. Welcome to JAC Designs."

"Good morning and thank you." I gave him a smile back.

"Follow me and I'll take you to Joe's office. As soon as he's gone in a couple of days, it's all yours and you can decorate it however you like."

"I get my own office?"

"Yeah. All the architects here do. You didn't have one of your own before?"

"No. I had a cubicle."

"Well, that's unfortunate. Here at JAC Designs, you get your own office." He grinned.

Before heading to Joe's office, Jake took me on a tour. He showed me where the bathrooms were located and the coffee/break room. He introduced me one by one to the staff and then he took me to the human resources department and waited for me while I signed a few papers. When we reached Joe's office, Jake introduced us and then left me in the care of him so he could fill me in on the projects he was working on. For the first time in a long time, I forgot about everything else going on in my life and just focused on my new job. It was refreshing and everyone was so nice. I knew I was going to like working here.

Later that afternoon, as Joe and I were going over things, I heard someone say my name.

"Charlotte?"

I looked up and saw Jim Yearns and Jake standing in the doorway.

"Jim?" I smiled as I walked over to him.

"What on earth are you doing here?" he asked as he hugged me.

"I work here now."

"You two know each other?" Jake asked with confusion.

"Of course we do. This little lady and I spent a lot of time together back in Seattle. She was your biggest competition, Jake. She designed that beautiful building I still can't stop thinking about."

"Wait a minute," I spoke. "You chose him over me?" I laughed. "Jim, I thought we were friends."

"I'm ashamed to say I did. He's a convincer, this one. How the hell did you end up here? Did your husband get transferred again?"

I swallowed hard.

"No. I left him and filed for divorce."

"What? Why? The last time we talked, you were so happy and singing his praises."

I stood there as tears began to fill my eyes. No. I wasn't doing this. I needed to be strong. And I needed to get used to telling people the truth, no matter how bad it hurt.

"That was before I found out he was cheating on me with some blonde bimbo from New York."

"Oh gee, Char. I'm so sorry. You don't deserve that. Damn. Do you want me to go and kick his ass for you?"

"Thanks, Jim, but I got my revenge, sort of. I burned all his clothes and broke some very valuable and sentimental things of his before I left Seattle. Now he's suing me for fifty thousand dollars for emotional distress and damages." I smiled when all I wanted to do was break down and cry.

"Good for you! I always knew you were a fighter. Hey, I have an idea. Jake, I want you and Charlotte to work together and redesign my building."

"What?" Jake said. "You're kidding, right?"

"Nope. I don't kid around when it comes to my projects. I loved your design and I loved hers and now, I want pieces of both brought together. God, this is like Christmas." He grinned. "I'll expect the new design in a week. That's enough time, right? Of course it is." He shook Jake's hand. "I'll be in touch soon." He turned to me and gave me a hug. "Keep your head up and forget about that asshole. You're much better off without him. You're in the right place now, kiddo." He gave me a wink.

"Thanks, Jim."

"You are a smart man hiring this one." He smiled as he looked at Jake and then headed down the hallway.

Jake and I stared at each other for a moment.

"Do you have your design?" he asked.

"Yeah. I do. I just didn't get around to putting it in my portfolio. I have it on my computer at home."

"You know, neither of us have the time to redesign that building. At least not here in the office with everything else going on, and you're just getting up to speed on Joe's projects. We're going to have to do it after work. I can swing by your place or you can come to my house."

"When?" I nervously asked.

"We should get started tonight since he's only given us a week."

"I can come by your house after work. I'll just run home and grab my laptop first."

"Great. Okay. I'll whip us up some dinner."

"You don't have to do that, Jake."

"We have to eat, Charlotte. It's no trouble at all. I'm a pretty good cook. I make a mean burger." He smirked. "Do you eat burgers?"

"I do." I bashfully smiled. "I'll bring the beer."

"Now you're talking." He grinned. "Okay. I'll text you my address and see you around seven?"

"Okay. I'll see you then."

❦

Jake

I inhaled a sharp breath as I walked down the hallway to my father's office with my hand tucked into my pants pocket. I couldn't believe she agreed to come to my house tonight. But we really didn't have a choice. We needed to get a jump-start on Jim's new design and there was no way we could start from scratch here in the office during regular work hours. Burgers? What the hell was I thinking? I could have done better than that.

"Dad, you have a minute?" I asked as I popped my head into his office.

"Sure, son. Come in."

"You know how Jim was just here?"

"Yeah."

"Apparently, he knows Charlotte. Her design was our competition."

"Well, I'll be dammed."

"He saw her and is thrilled she's working for us. He also said now that she's here, he wants her and me to start from scratch and design a new building together, taking components from my design and hers and blending them."

"You're kidding. We don't have time for that."

"I know, so she's coming to my house tonight and I'm going to look over hers and we're going to figure out a quick way to merge specific parts of each design."

"It's her first day. I don't want the poor girl overwhelmed."

He sat there and narrowed his eye at me for a moment.

"What?" I asked.

"She's a beautiful woman."

"I know she is. And?"

"Nothing. Do what you have to do to keep Jim happy. He has a lot of friends in high places he can recommend us to."

14

harlotte

I stepped into my apartment, changed into more comfortable clothing, and grabbed my laptop. I sat down on the edge of my bed and held it tightly against my chest. I couldn't believe I was going to his house. He was handsome with his six-foot-two stature, short brown hair, and brown eyes that reminded me of a pool of liquid chocolate. The five o'clock shadow he sported on his masculine jawline was trimmed to perfection. But the one thing that really got me, was every time he smiled, he had a cute little dimple on each side of his cheeks. It didn't matter, though. He could be the hottest and sexiest man on earth, which he was, and I still wouldn't be interested. It was going to take me a long time to ever be able to trust a man again, if I even could.

I was driving down the highway to Marina Del Rey when my phone rang.

"Hey, sis," I answered.

"How was your first day of work?"

"It was good. I think I'm really going to like it there."

"I knew you would. Aren't you home yet? You sound like you're in the car."

"I'm actually on my way to Jake's house."

"What? Why?"

"Long story short. A client wants me and Jake to design his building together. He was a potential client of mine back in Seattle. He loved my design but ended up going with JAC Designs. He saw me there today and wants us to start from scratch. So I'm going over there tonight so we can get a jumpstart on it."

"Good, I'm happy you're getting out, even if it is for work. Let me know how it goes."

"I will."

"Dinner is at my place next Saturday night for Mom and Dad's anniversary. I thought it would be nice to cook a special dinner for them instead of going out."

"I'll be there."

I pulled up to his house. 5205 Ocean Front. Wow. I grabbed my laptop and the beer from the front seat and walked up to the door. Before I had a chance to knock, it opened, and Jake stood there smiling.

"I heard you pull up," he spoke. "Come in." He gestured with his hand.

"Thank you."

"Here, let me take that." He grabbed the beer and I followed him into the kitchen.

"I am in love with the design of this house," I said as I looked around.

"Thanks. Would you like a tour?"

"I'd love one." I grinned.

He led me around the three-thousand-square-foot, three-bedroom, three-bath home with the cathedral ceilings and floor-to-ceiling windows throughout. Walls were painted in the color alabaster with washed oak trim and matching floor. Everything about the house was light, airy, and decorated to perfection. Did I mention that there were ocean views from every angle of the home? It was absolutely stunning, and I was in awe of the architectural style. He took me up to the rooftop, which housed a large deck overlooking the ocean.

"This is beautiful," I said as I leaned over the railing. "How long have you lived here?"

"Thanks. About five years," he replied as he stood next to me.

"Hey, Charlotte." Jake's father waved up to us.

"Is that your dad?"

"Yes." He sighed.

"Hello, Mr. Collins." I waved.

"Did I mention that my parents live two houses down?"

"No." I laughed. "Seriously?"

"Let's go back downstairs. I need to get the burgers on the grill. Yeah, and I'm serious about my parents. My grandfather was the original owner of the properties, and when he passed away, my father inherited them. The houses at the time were really old, and the property values kept increasing, so he demolished the houses, designed new ones, and had them built."

"How many does he own?" I asked.

"Six. Starting with mine and going down the beach."

He grabbed two bottles of beer from the fridge, took the cap off mine, and handed it to me with a smile.

"Thanks." The corners of my mouth curved upwards.

I followed him out to the patio as he put the burgers on the grill.

"Can I help with anything? I feel bad for just watching you."

"Nope. Everything else is already done."

I bit down on my bottom lip as I stood against the patio railing and watched him flip the burgers. I swallowed hard as I found myself thinking about him in ways I shouldn't have been. My phone rang, and when I pulled it from my jeans pocket, I noticed it was a Seattle number.

"Hello," I answered, and Jake turned and looked at me.

"Mrs. Foster?"

"Yes. Who's this?"

"My name is Ben and I'm calling from the Verizon store. Your husband is in here trying to upgrade his phone, and since the account is in your name, I'm going to need your pin number and authorization to do so."

"Does he know you're calling me?" I asked.

"No. He came in here with an attitude and started ranting and raving when I told him we needed to call you. So I told him I had to speak with the manager first."

"Please cancel that phone and number and remove it from my account."

"Are you sure? We'll have to charge you a cancellation fee since you're still in the middle of the contract."

"That's fine. I'll pay the cancellation fee. Trust me, it'll be worth every single penny."

"Okay, then. Have a good evening."

"You too, and if you're smart, you'll have security on standby first before you tell him."

"Thanks for the heads up."

"Thank you for calling, Ben."

I ended the call and sighed.

"Is everything okay?" Jake asked as he took the burgers off the grill.

"Yeah. I just cancelled my soon-to-be ex-husband's phone. Apparently, he's in the store now and wanting to upgrade. The nerve of him. First he cheats on me, then he's suing me for fifty thousand dollars in damages and emotional distress and he thinks he can upgrade his phone that's in my name? Who the hell does he think he is? Oh my God, I'm so sorry. I didn't mean to go on a rant like that."

"Don't apologize. You did the right thing, and you can feel free to rant to me anytime you want. I've been told I'm a pretty good listener." He winked and my belly did a flip.

He handed me the burgers and asked me to set them on the table while he grabbed the roasted potatoes from the oven and the Caesar salad he made from the fridge.

"I can't believe you made all this. You didn't have to go to all this trouble."

"It was no trouble at all. I love food and I love to cook."

"You did a great job. Thank you." I gave him a tender smile.

"You're welcome. Now we better hurry up and eat so we can get to work on that design for Jim."

15

Charlotte

After we finished eating, I helped Jake clean up and then I grabbed my laptop and brought up my design. He brought his chair closer to mine, and for some reason, my heart started racing. Maybe it was from the two beers I downed. Or maybe it was because there was something about him that made me feel different.

"Wait a minute," he spoke as he got up from his seat. "We can't do this design without having dessert."

"None for me. I'm way too full," I spoke.

"Too full for key lime pie?" He grinned as he held it up in front of me.

My jaw dropped as I stared at it.

"Key lime pie is my favorite."

"I know, and it's mine too. Slice?" he asked as his brow arched.

"Definitely." I smiled. "How did you know that it's my favorite?"

"Jillian told me."

"What?" I laughed as I looked at him. "Why would she tell you that?"

"I ran into her at the grocery store one day. I was picking up some steaks because my friend Chandler was coming by and she was at the bakery section. She told me that she was picking up a key lime pie for her sister with the hopes that it would help her feel a little better."

"I guess she told you a lot about me." My brows furrowed.

"Not really. She just said some things during our conversations. Neither one of us would have ever imagined that you'd be working for me."

"I guess."

He set our slices of pie down on the table and then took his seat.

"Did you make this?" I smirked.

"No." He chuckled. "There wasn't time. But, trust me, I'm going to learn how to make one. In fact, maybe one day we can make one together."

I could feel the heat rise in my cheeks as I bashfully took a bite. He studied my design and I studied his.

"I can see why Jim loved this so much. I love how you added the arches here." He pointed.

We worked together for a couple of hours and came up with a rough sketch. I glanced at my watch and saw that it was already midnight.

"I better go. It's already midnight. I honestly didn't think it was that late."

"I didn't either. We can go over the rest of it tomorrow," he said. "Maybe over lunch."

"Sounds good. I look forward to it."

I got up from my chair, grabbed my purse, and Jake followed me to the door.

"Be careful driving home."

"I will. Thanks again for dinner and for the pie. It was delicious."

"You're welcome. Can you do me a favor?"

"Sure. What is it?" I asked.

"Just shoot me a text message when you get home so I know that you arrived safely. It's really late and all."

"I will." I gave him a slight nod.

The whole way home, I felt anxious and I didn't know why. I felt like I couldn't calm the hell down. I took in a deep breath as I pulled into a parking space and went up to my apartment. Setting my purse on the table by the front door, I kicked off my shoes and then pulled out my phone.

"I'm home."

"Good. Thanks for letting me know. Good night, Charlotte. Sleep well."

"Good night, Jake."

&

The next morning when I walked into my office, I found my sister sitting behind my desk.

"Pretty fancy." She smiled.

"Thanks. I can't believe I have my own office. I feel so professional now." I smirked. "What are you doing here?"

"I have a meeting with Jake. He's on the phone right now, so I thought I'd come take a look at where my baby sister is going to be spending her days. How did it go last night?"

"It went good. He grilled us some burgers, made roasted potatoes, a Caesar salad, and bought a key lime pie for dessert. By the way, thanks for telling him everything about my personal life, including my favorite dessert."

"How did I know you'd end up working for him? Did the two of you get any work done? By the sounds of it, all you did was eat."

"Yes." I laughed. "We got the rough sketch done."

"What time did you get home?"

"About twelve thirty."

The corners of her mouth slowly curved upwards.

"What is that look for?"

"What look? I'm not giving you a look."

"Jillian, I'm ready. Good morning, Charlotte." Jake smiled.

"Good morning, Jake."

"Lunch today and Jim's design for a bit?"

"Sure. Sounds good."

The smile never left Jillian's face as she stared at me while she walked out with Jake. I rolled my eyes and sat down. Logging in to my computer, I brought up the first project I needed to tackle.

16

*J*ake

"So Charlotte told me she went over to your place last night to redesign some building?"

"Yeah. There just isn't any time for the both of us here at the office with everything else going on. Especially now that she has to take over Joe's projects and a few of them are close to the deadline."

"How did it go?"

"It went well. We successfully got the rough sketch done."

"Was she okay?" she asked.

"What do you mean?"

"Like was she acting normal, depressed, not very talkative?"

I couldn't help but let out a light laugh.

"She was perfectly fine. We had a good time."

"Good. I'm happy to hear that. She needs to get her life back."

"And she will on her own time. I don't think you need to worry so much about her."

"I can't help it. She's my baby sister. I've been helping take care of her since the day she was born."

I gave her a small smile and we got to work on the merger. By time we were finished, it was around lunch time, so I walked down to Charlotte's office to see what she was doing.

"Hey." I smiled as I stood in the doorway. "Do you like Chinese food?"

"Hi." She smiled back. "Yes. Why?"

"I was going to have Natasha place a lunch order for us. What do you like?"

"Kung Pao chicken sounds good."

"Kung Pao chicken it is. I'll have her order it now, and as soon as it gets here, we can go in the conference room."

"Okay. Just let me know." Her eyes stared into mine.

I gave her a slight nod and walked over to Natasha's desk.

"I need you to place a delivery order for lunch from the Chinese place down the street. Get an order of Kung Pao chicken, General Tso's chicken, and two egg rolls. Order something for yourself as well. Charlotte and I will be eating in the conference room while we work on Jim's design."

"Will do, boss. I really like Charlotte. She's very sweet." She smiled.

"I like her too." I winked as I walked back in my office.

The food was delivered, and Natasha set up the conference room for us. Grabbing my laptop, I walked down to Charlotte's office to let her know. When I approached the doorway, she was on the phone.

"Thanks for letting me know." She hung up the phone and looked at me.

"Lunch is here."

"Okay," she spoke in a somber voice.

I could tell that phone call upset her, but I didn't want to ask her what it was about. It was none of my business, and even though it upset me to see her upset, I needed to respect her privacy. We walked into the conference room and sat down next to each other in front of my lap top.

"I got you an egg roll." I handed it to her. "You like them, right?"

"Thank you. Yes, I do." She lightly smiled, but I could see the tears forming in her eyes.

"Are you okay?"

"I'm fine."

I pulled up the design and we worked on it some more while we ate our lunch.

§

*I*t was about eight o'clock when I received a phone call from Charlotte.

"Hello."

"Are you home? I had an idea for the design I can't get out of my head."

Suddenly, there was a knock at my door.

"Yeah. I'm home. Come on over and we can talk about it."

I walked over to the door, opened it, and smiled when I saw Charlotte standing there.

"I was already in the area," she spoke as she held the phone up to her ear.

I ended the call with a smile and invited her in.

"How about a glass of wine?"

"I'd love some," she said.

I poured us each a glass and I grabbed my laptop from my office and brought it over to the couch and sat down next to her. I brought up the design and she told me what changes she thought we could make.

"I like that idea. Very cool. Jim's going to love this." I grinned.

"Do you mind if I pour another glass?" she asked.

"No. Go right ahead."

I could tell she was still upset from earlier. After she poured some wine in her glass, she leaned over the counter, placed her face in her hands, and began to cry.

"I'm sorry," she said.

"What's wrong?" I walked over and clasped her shoulders from behind.

"My lawyer called, and we have to go to court in two weeks for the divorce and the lawsuit."

"Already?" I asked.

"The divorce is simple because there's nothing to split. According to my lawyer, we're going to kill two birds with one stone."

"That's good, though. Once you put this behind you, you can start living your life in peace."

"I know."

"Then why are you crying?" I asked as I removed my hands from her shoulders.

"Because this wasn't how my life was supposed to be. This wasn't in my plan."

"Life doesn't always go according to plan, Charlotte."

"But for me, it was supposed to. I wrote it out in my journal. I wrote my perfect life when I was eight years old. I'm twenty-six years old, married for seven months, and now I'm getting divorced. What twenty-six-year-old can say she's been married and divorced?"

"I think you'd be surprised how many people at that age are divorced. I have a friend named Emily who I went to high school with. She's twenty-nine and she's been divorced twice. And she has four kids."

"Seriously?" She turned around to face me and wiped the tears from her eyes.

"Yeah, seriously."

"I'm so embarrassed right now. I can't believe I'm doing this."

"Why? This isn't the first time I've seen you cry." I smiled at her.

"True. But we were strangers, so it didn't matter."

"Listen, Charlotte." I gripped her shoulders. "You have every right to be upset, torn apart, heartbroken, and distraught. It doesn't make you weak, and when you get through this, you're going to come out of it stronger than ever."

Her teary eyes stared into mine. The only thing I wanted to do was hold her and take away her pain. She didn't deserve this. She softly ran her finger across my lips before gently brushing hers against them. I returned her kiss with pleasure as I placed my hands on each side of her face.

"Don't judge me," she whispered as she broke our kiss.

"I would never judge you."

Our lips met again, eager to please as her fingers grasped the bottom of my shirt and she lifted it over my head. Our eyes met as she placed her hands firmly on my chest. My cock was already hard and desperately wanting to be buried deep inside her.

"Are you sure?" I asked as I stroked her cheek. "I don't want you to have any regrets."

"I'm sure and I won't regret anything."

I swooped down, picked her up, and carried her up to my bedroom.

17

*C*harlotte
His body was every woman's desire, strong and carved. His tongue glided across my slick opening, sending an intense burning desire throughout my body. Every soft stroke and circle motion he made brought me closer to a fulfilling orgasm. My fingers tangled in his hair as he explored me, and my back arched at the pleasure that tore through me. Soft, sexual moans escaped my lips, making me forget about the chaos in my life and only focusing on this moment.

He groaned as the wetness dripped from me and he softly kissed his way up to my lips. His strong body hovered over me as his cock pushed its way inside, inch by inch. He moved in and out of me slowly while our lips twisted with pleasure. The buildup was coming as my legs tightened around him. He gasped as he felt my body tremble and halted while he exploded inside me. Our breathing was erratic as he lowered his body on me and I could feel the rapid beating of his heart. He rolled off me and removed the condom. I lay there, trying to catch my breath as my body still trembled.

"Are you okay?" he asked with a smile as his finger circled around my shoulder.

"Yeah. Just trying to catch my breath."

"Stay here tonight. You've been drinking and I don't want you driving home."

"I had two glasses of wine." I laughed.

"I still would like you to stay."

I stared into his pleading eyes.

"Jake, I don't want to make things complicated. You're my boss and we already crossed the line."

"I'm your boss at work, but here, off the clock, I'm just an ordinary man who wants you to stay the night."

"We have work in the morning," I said.

"And we'll get up early and then you can go home and change. But if you can't or don't want to, I understand."

He was so damn sexy, and I was finding it hard to resist him.

"I snore," I said.

The corners of his mouth curved upwards.

"Me too."

"I have a habit of stealing all the covers."

"Take them all. I don't care."

"I've never slept next to any other man than Alex."

"Then let me be your first." He slowly stroked my cheek.

"Well, since you've convinced me to stay, can I have another glass of wine?" I smiled.

"Coming right up."

He climbed out of bed, pulled his underwear on, and left the bedroom. A few moments later, he walked back in with two glasses and the bottle of opened wine.

"Your wine, Madame." He grinned.

"Thank you. Can I ask you a personal question?"

"Of course. You can ask me anything."

"How long were you with your ex-girlfriend?"

"About a year."

"Any idea why she would cheat on you?"

"No. But things with us weren't always good. She liked to start a lot of arguments over nothing and she always had to be right about everything."

"Why did you stay with her for that long, then?"

"I don't know, Charlotte. I really don't. Maybe it was out of convenience. Maybe I was just settling because my parents expected me to start thinking about settling down. My best friend, Chandler, couldn't stand her and they were always arguing about something. I'd like you to meet him. I know he'd really like you."

I gave him a small smile as I sipped on my wine.

"Maybe we should get some sleep. It's late," I spoke.

"Good idea."

He lay down and held out his arm. I set my wine glass down on the nightstand and snuggled against him. Fear started to rise inside me as it felt too right being in his arms.

Ja

ake

I lay there, and as I held her, things never felt so right. Making love to her was the best thing that had happened to me in a very long time. She was perfect and I was falling for her more every day. But I knew that it was going to take a lot of work on my part to make her see that I wasn't like her soon-to-be ex-husband. To make her see that I was trustworthy and honest. Even though I hadn't known her very long, every time I looked at her, I saw a future with us in it.

C

harlotte

I opened my eyes and forgot for a moment where I was. Last night had been a weak moment and now regret had settled inside me. *Shit.* I looked at the clock and it was four a.m. Carefully getting out of bed, I grabbed my clothes and my shoes and tiptoed out of the room. After haphazardly putting them on, I grabbed my purse and quietly slipped out the door. I climbed in my car and pulled away as fast as I could. How was I going to face him at the office? How was I going to tell him that what happened last night couldn't happen again? My life was already a mess and I didn't need the complications of another man to add to it.

The moment I stepped inside my apartment, I made a cup of coffee, took a shower, and got ready for work. As I was brushing out my hair, my phone dinged with a text message from Jake. Instantly, my stomach twisted in a knot.

"*Good morning. Why did you leave so early?*"

"*Good morning. I couldn't sleep, so I thought I might as well go home and get ready for work.*"

"*I missed seeing you when I woke up. I'll see you soon at the office.*"

I didn't respond because I didn't know what to say. My heart ached at the thought that I led him on. I needed to talk to Jillian.

"You're an early bird this morning," she answered.

"Yeah. I guess so."

"What's wrong? I can tell by your tone something upset you."

I put her on speaker and set my phone down while I finished doing my hair.

"Jillian, my life is so fucked up right now."

"What happened?"

"Please don't be mad at me."

"Sis, it's too early for this. What did you do?"

"Promise me you won't be mad."

"The only way I'll be mad is if you tell me you're going back to Alex."

"Ugh. How could you even say that?"

"Okay then. I won't be mad. What did you do?"

I swallowed hard and then took in a deep breath.

"I had sex with Jake last night."

"Are you serious? Jesus, Charlotte, good for you! How was he? I bet he was amazing! I knew you liked him."

"Jillian, stop! It was a mistake, a huge mistake, and now I have to see him this morning."

"Aren't you at his place now?"

"No. I snuck out at four a.m."

"You left without so much as a goodbye? Ugh, Char, that was a mistake. Sleeping with him wasn't."

"I never should have done it. I was drinking and had a weak moment."

"Weak moment or not, I'm proud of you," she spoke. "Listen, we'll have to chat later. I have to finish getting ready for work. I can't be late for my meeting with my boss. Chin up and don't worry about it. You did nothing wrong except have a good time, which is something you deserve."

I ended the call, finished my second cup of coffee, and headed out the door to work. As I was walking down the hallway to my office, I saw Jake walking towards me with a smile on his face.

"Good morning." He followed me into the office.

"Morning."

"Like I said in my text message, I missed seeing you when I woke up."

"Sorry about that. I didn't want to wake you. You were sleeping so peacefully."

He walked over to me and tenderly brushed his lips against mine.

"You're sweet." He smiled. "But I was only sleeping peacefully because you were lying next to me. Next time, don't leave without saying goodbye."

I gulped and then gave him a small smile.

"I have a meeting to get to. I'll talk to you later." He kissed my lips one last time before heading out the door.

18

Jake

 She regretted last night. I could tell or else she wouldn't have left my house. Plus, she was acting different this morning; a little standoff-ish. I knew this would happen and I should have stopped it, but I had wanted her so badly from the moment my eyes laid sight on her. The best thing to do now was to leave her alone and give her space. I really had no choice. If I pushed it, she'd end up hating me. She was going through hell and I wanted to be there for her. But for now, that wasn't an option. If she needed me, she'd let me know. From now on, the relationship between Charlotte Foster and me was strictly professional, no matter how much it killed me.

Later that afternoon, I had Natasha call her down to my office.

"You wanted to see me?" she asked.

"Yes. I need you to review the final design before we show it to Jim. I printed it out."

I got up from my seat and spread the long sheet of paper across the table in my office.

"I love it and I think he will too. It was a good idea bringing our two designs together."

"Okay. I'll give him a call and let him know it's ready for him to see. That's all," I spoke.

She turned and headed for the door and then she suddenly stopped.

"Jake?" She turned around and looked at me.

"Yes?"

"About last night."

"Charlotte, don't worry about it. It was nothing. We were drinking and things got out of control. It happens. It won't affect our working relationship."

"Sure. Okay. I'm glad we cleared that up. It was bothering me all day."

I gave her a smile and she turned and walked out the door. A few moments later, my office door flew open and Charlotte stepped back into my office.

"No. You're wrong."

"Wrong about what?" I asked.

"It *was* something. The reason I left at four a.m. was because I was ashamed. I had a weak moment yesterday and I was feeling down and sorry for myself. I used you, Jake, and I'm sorry."

I wanted to tell her that she could use me any time she wanted to.

"I'm a mess in every way possible and I'm trying so hard to put the pieces of my not-so-perfect life back together the best I can." Tears filled her eyes. "But I really value our friendship and I'd rather have you as a friend than not in my life at all."

I walked over and held her face in my hands as her beautiful brown eyes stared into mine.

"You don't have to worry. I'll always be your friend, and I understand. If there's anything you need, I'm here for you. Never forget that."

"Thank you. You have no idea how much that means to me," she softly spoke.

*a*fter I left the office, I stopped by Chandler's house to help him move some furniture down to the basement. Veronica, his girlfriend, moved in about a week ago and she decided it was time for some new furniture. Apparently, his looked too masculine. I walked into his house through the patio door like I always did and found Veronica in the kitchen unpacking some boxes.

"Getting all settled." I smiled as I walked inside.

"Hey, Jake. These are the last two boxes. They're just a few things I had over at my apartment. How are you?"

"I'm good."

"Chandler is upstairs changing. He'll be down in a second. Can I get you a beer?"

"That would be great. It's been a long day."

"I ordered pizza for you guys."

"Hey, bro." Chandler grinned as he walked into the kitchen. "Let's eat first. I'm starving."

As we took a seat at the table, there was a knock on the door and Veronica went to answer it.

"That must be her flaky friend Gemma," he spoke.

"Isn't she the psychic?" I asked.

Chandler rolled his eyes. "Yeah, sure."

I let out a chuckle and the two of them walked into the kitchen.

"Hello, Chandler," Gemma said.

"How you doing, Gemma?"

"Good. Thanks."

"Gemma, this is Jake, Chandler's best friend. Jake, this is Gemma."

"Nice to meet you, Gemma." I extended my hand.

"Likewise, Jake." She lightly shook it and held it strangely for a moment.

"Don't mind us, Gemma is going to smudge the house."

"What?" Chandler asked as he turned around and looked at her.

"She's smudging the house with sage. Since I live here now, it needs to be cleansed."

He sighed and rolled his eyes. I couldn't help but let out a light laugh. We finished eating and I helped Chandler move the couches down to the basement. When we got back upstairs, Gemma was walking around with a bundle of sage in her hand and chanting.

"That shit smells, Veronica," Chandler said.

"Shut up, Chandler."

He sighed as he went to the refrigerator and pulled out two bottles of beer.

"Thanks. I'm going to have to get going after this one," I said.

"What's wrong? You seem a little down today."

"Charlotte told me that she values our friendship and she'd rather have me as a friend than not in her life at all."

"Damn. I'm sorry." He placed his hand on my shoulder. "You know she's going through a lot right now."

"I know. It's just that after last night, I want her more than ever."

"Last night? Did you two—"

"Yeah, we did." I took a sip of my beer.

"And?" he asked.

"It was amazing. It was like we were connected on some deep level."

"Because you were," Gemma said as she walked past us. "Your souls were connected."

I glanced at her and then back at Chandler as he rolled his eyes.

"There's nothing I can do, Chandler. According to Charlotte, her life is a mess right now." I finished off my beer. "I have to go. Thanks for the beer and pizza."

"No problem, bro. Thanks for helping me with the furniture. Don't worry about Charlotte. She'll come around."

I gave him a small smile as I walked out the door.

19

C harlotte
　　It was Saturday and I spent most of the day lying in bed reading a self-help book. I hadn't really seen or talked to Jake in a week since we had our conversation. He had been in meetings and out of the office. The only time I saw him was for a brief second yesterday when he popped his head into my office and told me that we had a meeting with Jim Yearns on Monday morning, and then he was gone in a flash before the word "okay" could escape my lips.

I finally dragged myself out of bed, showered, and then headed out the door to my sister's house for my parents' anniversary dinner.

"Hey you." Chris smiled as he kissed my cheek.

"Hi, Chris," I said as I walked inside.

"Hello, sweetheart." My dad gave me a hug. "How's my baby girl doing?"

"I'm okay, Dad. Happy anniversary."

"Thank you. Your mom and sister are in the kitchen."

I walked into the kitchen and set the cake on the counter.

"Happy anniversary, Mom." I smiled as I gave her a hug.

"Thank you, darling."

"Grab a glass and pour yourself some wine," Jillian spoke.

"Is there anything I can help with?" I asked.

"Nope. I've got it all under control." She smiled.

As I was having a conversation with my mom, I heard a voice coming from the foyer.

"Is that Jake?" My brows furrowed as I looked at Jillian.

"Umm. Yeah. I needed him to stop by and sign a couple papers for the merger since I'm going to be out of town on Monday."

"Oh, I want to meet him," my mom said as she scurried out of the kitchen.

I followed behind her to make sure she didn't say anything embarrassing since she had a habit of doing that.

"Charlotte." Jake gave me a nod.

"Hi." I lightly smiled.

"Jake, it's so nice to finally meet you. I'm Linda, Jillian and Charlotte's mother."

"It's nice to meet you." He grinned as he shook her hand.

"Jake, why don't you stay for dinner?" Jillian spoke.

What the fuck was she doing?

"That's okay. I don't want to intrude."

"You wouldn't be intruding, dear," my mother said as she hooked her arm around his. "We want you to stay."

He glanced at me and I bit down on my bottom lip and shrugged. "Sorry," I mouthed.

"No isn't an option. We have plenty of food and you're already here," Jillian said.

My mother took Jake into the living room to meet my dad while I followed Jillian into the kitchen.

"What the hell are you doing?" I asked.

"What? He's here, so he can join us."

"Do you know how awkward this is for me?"

"Why? You work together. You see each other all day, every day."

"I told him that I like him as a friend," I spoke through gritted teeth. "He hasn't really talked to me since."

"Well, you're being dumb. Get over it, Charlotte."

"Oh my God. Are you serious right now?"

Before she could say another word, my mom and Jake walked into the kitchen.

"I can't thank you enough for everything you've done for Charlotte, especially making sure she got home safely that night she decided to be reckless."

"Mom!"

"It was my pleasure," he said as he looked at me.

"So tell me about yourself," my mom casually said as she walked him back out of the kitchen.

"I just want to die right now. Thanks a lot, sis."

"You're overreacting. He's your boss, my client, and our friend. Plus, he's the guy who saved you that night. Something awful could have happened if that guy would have gotten you out of the bar. Jake got into a fight with him and stopped him."

"What?" I cocked my head at her.

"Dinner's ready. Help me bring it to the table. If you want to know more, ask him yourself."

I sat at the table in silence as everybody else talked. Jake sat next to me and I was feeling very uncomfortable. But nobody fucking cared how I felt. It was all about Jake and it pissed me off. After we ate, I helped clean up while Jake, Chris, and my dad went into the media room and played some pool.

"He is such a wonderful man," my mom said.

"Charlotte slept with him and then told him they can only be friends," my sister blurted out.

"JILLIAN!"

"Is that true, Charlotte?" my mom asked.

"I don't want to talk about this."

I grabbed my glass of wine and stepped out onto the patio.

"Hey," Jake spoke as he walked up next to me holding a bottle of beer.

"I'm sorry about all this," I said as I glanced over at him.

"What are you sorry for? Your family is amazing, and your dad is so funny. To be honest, I'm glad I stayed."

"I need you to tell me exactly what happened that night back in Seattle," I said.

"Why?"

"Because Jillian said something about some guy trying to get me out of the bar and you got into a fight with him. I want to know everything that happened."

"It doesn't matter, Charlotte."

"It matters to me, Jake."

"Fine. You were drunk and dancing on the dance floor when some guy approached you. He was touching you and then he grabbed your arm and tried to get you to go with him. I stepped in and told him to back off. I took hold of your arm, and as I was getting you out of there, he tapped me on the back and then punched me when I turned around. I punched him back and sent him to the ground."

"Were you hurt?"

"I had a bruise on my cheek. It was no big deal."

"Then what?"

"I took you home, and when I got you inside, you told me you were going to be sick, so I hurried and got you to the bathroom and held your hair back while you threw up."

"Oh my God." I placed my hand over my face.

"This is why I didn't want to tell you. You were already embarrassed enough."

"I'm such a damn mess." I shook my head.

"No, Charlotte, you're not. If you want my honest opinion, I think you're just perfectly you." He smiled.

"Hey, you two," Jillian said as she stepped out on the balcony. "It's time for Pictionary! Come inside."

"Pictionary?" Jake's brow raised as he looked at me.

"It's something we always play. You're on my team and we're going to smoke their asses." I grinned.

He let out a chuckle as we went back inside. When we walked into the living room, Jillian had the huge whiteboard set up and the game sitting on the coffee table.

"The teams will be as follows: Jake and Charlotte, me and Chris, Mom and Dad."

"Jill, that's not fair. Both Char and Jake are artists. One of them should be with one of us non-artist people," Chris spoke.

"Sucks to be you." I grinned at him.

We played for a couple of hours until my family couldn't take anymore. Jake and I had won every round and I couldn't remember when I had such a good time. We made a great team and there was a lot of laughter. I had a little too much to drink and was really feeling the effects of the alcohol. Jake could tell as he walked over to me.

"I think I'm going to drive you home," he said.

"I think that's a good idea."

20

*C*harlotte
Jake drove me home and came up to my apartment because he needed to use the bathroom. I kicked off my shoes and took a seat on the couch while I waited for him.

"Your apartment is really nice," he said as he emerged from the bathroom.

"Thanks. I like it here."

"Well, I better get going."

"Thank you for driving me home."

"You're welcome." The corners of his mouth slightly curved upwards.

"Not just for taking me home tonight, but for what you did for me back in Seattle. I know I can never say thank you enough. I was stupid and reckless and not thinking straight. I could have seriously been hurt if you weren't there and stepped in."

He walked over to the couch and sat down next to me.

"You were stupid and reckless, but you had every reason to be. You're human, Charlotte, and we humans tend to act like that a few times in our lives, especially when we've been hurt. The best thing you can do is consider it a lesson learned and forget about it."

I laid my head on his shoulder and he put his arm around me. I couldn't help it. All I wanted was to feel him close to me.

"I know I have no right to ask this, but will you stay with me tonight?"

"If that's what you really want," he spoke.

"It is. I just want to sleep next to you." I looked up at him.

"Then I'll stay." His lips gave way to a smile.

I lifted my head, got up from the couch, grabbed his hand, and walked him into my bedroom. He stripped out of his clothes while I was in the bathroom changing into my nightshirt and climbed under the covers. I climbed in and snuggled against him. His arms wrapped around me and the feeling of warmth and comfort took over. *Shit.* That wasn't the only feeling that took over. He smelled musky, woodsy, clean, citrusy, and sexy all rolled into one. It was a scent I'd been admiring all night. It was different from the other colognes he wore. It heightened my senses and the fire down below was roaring. His muscular chest was firm beneath my head and I couldn't help but run my fingers softly around his rock-hard abs while his fingers deftly stroked my hair.

I pressed my lips against his bare chest as my hand traveled down his torso and stopped when I reached his erection, which was protruding through his underwear. My fingers softly stroked him up and down as I heard the sharp intake of his breath.

"Charlotte," he whispered.

I climbed on top of him and stared into his eyes before leaning down and brushing my lips against his.

"I want you," I softly spoke.

"I want you too. I don't have a condom with me," he said as he brushed away a strand of my hair from my face.

"I'm on birth control. I don't mind if you don't."

"Are you sure?" he asked.

"I'm positive." I kissed his lips.

He reached down and pulled my nightshirt over my head, tossing it on the floor next to the bed. Our lips met once again as he rolled me on my back and hovered over me. His mouth devoured my neck as the flames inside me grew out of control. His hand traveled down to my panties as he successfully took them down and then dipped his finger inside me. I gasped at the pleasure and threw my head back. Moans fell from his lips as the wetness dripped from me. He removed his finger and his hands took hold of my breasts while his tongue traveled down below, forming tiny circles around every inch of my sweet spot. My hands tangled in his hair as delightful moans emerged from me.

"I love the way you sound," he softly spoke. "You have no idea how much it turns me on."

"Oh my God," I yelled. "Don't stop, Jake. Please, don't stop."

"Come for me, Charlotte. I want to taste more of you."

My body tightened as a powerful orgasm tore through me.

"I need you right now," he said as he smashed his mouth into mine and he thrust inside me. "Fuck, you feel so good. Oh my God," he moaned.

My arms tightened around him as he moved in and out of me at a rapid pace. He halted, flipped me over, and took me from behind as his hands firmly gripped my ass. Neither one of us were quiet about it and I was pretty sure my neighbors could hear. I didn't care. He felt so good inside me and it felt right. My body geared up for another orgasm as I gripped the comforter with my hands and released. After a few more thrusts, Jake halted and exploded while buried deep inside me. He slowly lowered his body against mine, stretched his arms out, and interlaced our fingers while we tried to regain our breath.

"That was—"

"I know it was." I smiled with the slight turn of my head and looked back at him.

He brought his lips to mine before climbing off me and rolling onto his back. He held his arm out and I snuggled against him, placing my head on his chest. His fingers lightly stroked my shoulder as mine stroked his chest.

"I'm here for you, Charlotte. Never forget that," he said.

I pressed my lips against his chest and closed my eyes.

᠀

he next morning, I was awoken by several knocks on my
door. After climbing out of bed and throwing on my robe, I
went over to the peephole, saw it was Jillian, and opened the door.

"For fuck sakes, Jill. Do you want to wake the whole building up?"

"It's eleven o'clock. I brought bagels." She grinned as she held up
the bag and stepped inside.

"Now really isn't a good time," I said as I didn't want her to know
that Jake spent the night.

"Why? What are you doing? It looks to me like you just rolled out
of bed."

"Oh. Good morning," Jake awkwardly spoke as he emerged from
the bedroom.

"Oh shit. Did I interrupt something?" she asked with a sly smile.

"No. You didn't," I said as I grabbed three plates from the cabinet.

"Well then," she smiled at him, "good morning. Bagel?"

"Actually, I'm going to get going."

He walked into the bedroom and grabbed the rest of his clothes. I
followed behind.

"You don't have to leave," I said.

He turned to me and placed his hands firmly on my hips.

"I know I don't, but I want to shower and change clothes. Are you
doing anything today?"

"No. I don't think so."

"Then how about spending the day with me on my boat?"

"I didn't know you had a boat." I grinned.

"I do and it's a big boat." He winked.

"I'd love to."

"Great. I'll be back to pick you up in a couple of hours." He kissed
my lips.

He walked out of the room, said goodbye to Jillian, and left my
apartment.

"So..." she slowly spoke.

"Don't. I don't want to talk about it."

"Too bad. I caught you in the act. It's time to confess your sins, little sister."

I walked over to the Keurig and made us each a cup of coffee to have with our bagel.

"There's nothing to confess. He drove me home and shit happened. What can I say?"

"You wanted it. Admit it." Her eye narrowed at me.

"So what if I did?"

The corners of her mouth curved upwards into a cunning grin.

"You're moving on and I'm so proud of you."

"Ugh, Jill." I placed my hands on my head. "I feel like such a bad person."

"Why? You like Jake and there's nothing wrong with that."

"I'm still married."

"Oh please. Do you think that douchebag was thinking about that when he was sticking his dick in someone else's V?"

"Thanks a lot." I cocked my head at her.

"I'm not going to apologize for being raw and real with you. Alex is a dick. He always has been and he always will be. It's time you saw him for what he really is."

"I know that, but the wound is still fresh and open."

"You're not using Jake as a band-aid, are you?"

"What do you mean?" I asked as I took a bite of my bagel.

"You know exactly what I mean, Char. Are you using him to help heal and close your wound?"

"No! Of course not."

"Well, I hope you aren't because he's an amazing man and he doesn't deserve that."

She was really starting to piss me off with her words.

"I need to go take a shower. Thanks for the bagels," I said as I got up from the table.

"Char, don't be mad."

"I'm not." I put my hand up on my way to the bathroom.

"Yes you are! You gave me the hand!"

21

Jake

After going home and showering, I climbed back into my car and headed over to Charlotte's apartment. Spending the night with her was everything to me and I knew spending the day with her was going to be even better. Being careful wasn't an option anymore. I was already too far in with her.

"Hi." She smiled as she opened the door.

"Hi. You look amazing. Are you ready?"

"Thanks. Yeah, just let me grab my purse."

We climbed into my car, and as we were driving to the marina, I reached over and took hold of her hand. I wasn't sure if it was such a good idea or how she'd react, but she graciously held it and I couldn't have been happier. We pulled into the marina, climbed out of the car, and I led her to my boat.

"Here she is."

"This? This isn't a boat. This is a yacht." She smiled.

"Did I not mention that?" I smirked.

"No. All you said was that you had a big boat." She laughed.

"Good afternoon, Mr. Collins."

"Good afternoon, Giles. This is Charlotte and she'll be accompanying me today."

"It's nice to you meet you, Charlotte."

"And you as well, Giles."

"I have appetizers on the deck for you with a bottle of champagne chilling."

"Thank you, Giles. I appreciate it." I patted his shoulder.

"You have a personal yacht chef?" Her brow arched.

"Only on special occasions. Come on. I'll show you around and then we'll set sail."

After we set sail, we went up on the deck and filled our plates with the delicious appetizers that Giles prepared for us.

"This is really nice. Thank you for inviting me," Charlotte spoke.

"Thank you for coming." I tenderly kissed her lips.

"Can I ask you a question?" she asked as we sat down in the comfy lounge chairs.

"Of course you can."

"Why did you name your boat *Sadie's Star*?"

"I named it after my sister. She passed away when she was ten years old from leukemia."

"I'm so sorry, Jake. I had no idea."

"One night about a month before she passed away, we were on our parents' boat and we were lying on the deck looking up at the stars. She pointed to one that was bigger and brighter than the others. She told me that when she dies, she will always be watching over me in the sky and that all I needed to do was look up and find the star that stood out and that would be her. That's why I named the boat after her. Sometimes, when it's dark and I'm having a bad day, I'll take the boat out and stare up at the sky as the wind sweeps across my face, and every single time, there's one bigger and brighter star up there." I smiled.

She reached over and grabbed my hand.

"I miss her. She was so full of life, and even when she was diagnosed and going through chemo, she never let it get her down. She was always so positive when the rest of us were falling apart."

"She sounds like she was a wonderful person," she said.

"She was. She was my baby sister, and even though there was a six-year age difference between us, we were very close, and I wanted nothing more than to protect her."

Charlotte reached over and kissed my cheek.

"You're a good man, Jake Collins." She smiled.

We spent the rest of the day on the boat talking, getting to know each other better, eating, and watching the sunset over the ocean. I couldn't remember the last time I had such an incredible day.

She stood at the railing as I stood behind her with my arms wrapped around her waist.

"The sunset is so beautiful," she spoke.

"It is. It's one of my favorite parts of the day." I lightly pressed my lips against her shoulder.

She brought her hand around and placed it on the back of my neck as she tilted her head to the side while my lips softly stroked the flesh of her neck. She turned around in my arms and our lips softly met. Her arms wrapped around my neck as we stared into each other's eyes. While our lips tangled, I picked her up and carried her to the bedroom, where we spent the next hour making love.

"I never had sex on a yacht before." She grinned as she lay on her side staring at me.

"Then I'm happy that my yacht was your first." I smirked as I traced her lips with my finger. "We should get dressed. It's getting late and I should get you home. We have that early morning meeting tomorrow with Jim."

"I sure hope he likes what we did," she said.

"He's going to love it." I smiled as I kissed her lips and climbed out of bed.

I drove her back to her apartment and walked her to the door. What I wouldn't give for this day not to end.

"Thank you for a wonderful day," she spoke as she grabbed hold of my hands.

"You're welcome. Thank you for spending it with me."

The corners of her mouth curved upwards into a bashful smile. I leaned in and softly brushed my lips against hers, kissing her good night.

"I'll see you in the morning. Sleep well," I said.

"You too, Jake."

I climbed into my car, and as I was driving home, my phone rang. It was my dad calling.

"Hey, Dad," I answered.

"Hello, son. Are you in the car?"

"Yeah. I just dropped Charlotte off at her apartment and I'm heading home."

"Oh. Why were you with Charlotte on a Sunday?"

"I took her on my yacht for the day."

"Am I to assume you two are growing closer?"

I couldn't help but smile when he said that.

"Yeah, Dad. I think we are."

"Just be careful, Jake. She's still going through a lot and I don't want you to get hurt."

"I'm a big boy, Dad. Anyway, is there a reason you called?"

"Yeah. I just got off the phone with Jim Yearns. He said he tried to get hold of you earlier, but his calls weren't going through. He had to fly back to Seattle for a family emergency and he won't be back until sometime next week. He needs to reschedule the meeting."

"Okay. I'll let Charlotte know. Thanks, Dad."

*C*harlotte

 The moment I walked into my apartment, I kicked off my shoes and threw myself back on the bed. Looking up at the ceiling, I thought about Jake and the past couple of days. I felt things for him. Feelings that were unfamiliar to me because I thought I had felt everything there was to feel with Alex. I thought about how Jake saved me that night in Seattle. Did I feel a sense of obligation to him for what he'd done? My mind was like a prison where doubt, anger, fear, and self-hatred resided. I was scared because trust was such an issue for me now and I would carry that into future relationships. Jake was perfect as far as I was concerned and he didn't need the fucked-up, imperfect me with all of my emotional baggage. He deserved better. He deserved someone who could give him everything he wanted and needed without all the bullshit attached to it. I wished I could be that someone, but I couldn't, and I needed to tell him.

 The next morning, after setting my things down in my office, I walked to the break room to grab a cup of coffee and saw Jake standing there pouring himself a cup.

 "Good morning," I spoke.

"Good morning, beautiful." He smiled.

I swallowed hard as I grabbed a cup and poured some coffee into it.

"Our meeting with Jim needed to be rescheduled. He had to fly back to Seattle for a family emergency."

"Oh no. I hope everything is okay."

"I don't know the details. He'll be in touch when he gets back to L.A. How about dinner tonight?" he asked.

I could feel the churning in my belly and the dread that seeped into my veins.

"I actually have plans tonight," I lied.

"Okay." He gently smiled. "Another night, then."

"Excuse me, Jake?" Natasha spoke as she stopped in the doorway of the break room. "Mr. Kearney is on the phone for you. He says it's an emergency." She rolled her eyes.

Jake sighed. "Thanks, Natasha. Whatever you're doing tonight, I hope you have a good time." He smiled as he walked out.

I slowly closed my eyes as guilt washed over me. He was too nice of a guy and the last thing I wanted to do was hurt him. Later that night, after I got home from work, I changed my clothes and walked down to the beach. My toes nestled themselves in the warm sand as a light wind swept across my face. The waves rolled over the shore as the whispers of the ocean provided the peace I desperately sought inside me. I thought about Jake and how I lied to him. I hated myself and I couldn't shake the desolate feeling inside. I wasn't the girl who lied and what I did today was nothing short of the coward's way out. I sat myself down in the sand and gazed out into the blue ocean water as a tear fell down my cheek. Taking my phone from my pocket, I sent Jake a text message. It was now or never.

"I lied to you. I don't have plans tonight. But we need to talk."

"Okay. When and where?"

"I'm down at the beach by my apartment. Can you come here?"

"Of course. I'm on my way."

I brought my knees up to my chest as I wrapped my arms around them and took in a deep breath. How did my life get so fucked up in such a short period of time? I wasn't even divorced yet and here I was having to tell the man that I so deeply cared about that we couldn't be together. I was in deep thought as my heart was racing and Jake walked up and sat down next to me. I looked over at him and he could see the tears in my eyes.

"Before you say anything, Charlotte, there's something I want to tell you. I love you. I'm in love with you and I can't help it. I can't explain what happened the moment you looked up at me on the sidewalk back in Seattle. It was like a bolt of lightning went through me and I had never felt anything like that before."

"Jake, don't." I wiped my tears.

"I know you don't want to hear it, but I don't care. I'm done hiding my feelings for you. I know you're going through a lot and all I want to do is help you through it."

"You can't help me. The only person who can do that is me and I can't if we're together."

"Don't say that, Charlotte. You know damn well that what we have is undeniable. I know you feel it too."

"I don't know if I do. There's a part of me that feels an obligation to you for what you've done for me, and I don't know if what I feel is real or not."

"How can you say that?"

"It's the truth." I swallowed the hard lump in my throat. "Everything happened so fast. One minute, my life is thrown on the floor by Alex, and the next, it's being picked up by you. I don't even know who I am anymore. I spent the last ten years trying to build the perfect life and it was all a lie."

"And that was the past, Charlotte. You can't change what happened, but you can move forward and create a new life, a better life. Every day you wake up is a new beginning. I know your heart is broken, but all I ask is that you let me be the one to put all those broken pieces back together again." He reached over and wiped away my tears as I slowly closed my eyes.

"I don't love you, Jake."

Those were the hardest words I ever had to say and the little piece of my heart that was hanging by a string completely shattered with the rest of it.

"Do you really mean that?" he asked.

"Yes." I lied.

"Okay, Charlotte. I can't change how you feel, but I can leave you alone and let you live your life."

"I'm so sorry," I cried.

"So am I. Because I know we were made for each other and you know it too. You're just too scared to admit it because you're afraid to love anyone again. Not everyone is out to destroy you and not every love that comes your way will leave you heartbroken. I'm not Alex, Charlotte, and I never will be. I'm sorry that I have to say this, but our relationship from now on is strictly professional. I'm your boss and you're my employee and that's all we are. Nothing else."

The moment he got up and walked away, I placed my head between my legs and started sobbing. The pain I never wanted to feel again was back with a vengeance, rearing its ugly head and paralyzing me.

23

ONE WEEK LATER

*C*harlotte
When I opened the door, Jillian took one look at me and furrowed her brows.

"Why aren't you ready? I told you that I'd be here to pick you up at six thirty."

"I'm not going," I sadly spoke as I walked into the kitchen.

"Yes you are. We had this planned and you're getting out of this damn apartment."

She walked to my bedroom. A few moments later, she returned and threw one of my sundresses at me.

"Put this on now. You're going and that's the end of it."

"Jillian, I would really appreciate it if you just left me alone."

"Yeah, and I would appreciate it if you'd get your head out of your ass and stop with this pity party bullshit. It's Candace's birthday and she really wants you there. I love you to pieces, but tonight isn't about you. It's about Candance and this awesome little party I'm throwing her. So get your ass in your room and get dressed," she spoke in an authoritative tone. "You can go back to your little pity party when you get home."

I shot her a dirty look as I went into the bedroom and slammed the door like a child throwing a temper tantrum. This past week had been difficult at the office. Jake wouldn't even look at me and I didn't blame him. Our brief conversations consisted of a few moments of work-related things and it was hard. My court date was set for Monday morning at nine a.m. and having to see Alex again was slowly killing me inside. The last thing I wanted to do was go out. I'd done nothing since Jake and I talked. I went to work and then came home and went to bed. I barely ate and slept way more than any human should. I was depressed and sick to my stomach one hundred percent of the time.

I changed into my dress, ran a brush through my hair, touched up my makeup, and Jillian and I headed out the door and climbed into the limo bus to pick up the other girls and head to the Emerson Theater, a dance club on Hollywood Boulevard. Our party consisted of eight girls, including me and Jillian. They were my and Jillian's friends that we'd known since we were kids. They were Jillian's posse while growing up, but they always included me.

As I sipped on my cosmopolitan, I took a seat on the purple couch and people-watched. I didn't feel like dancing and I didn't feel like being social. But, for Candance, I put on a happy façade and tried to make the most of it. As people were dancing and having a good time, I glanced over at the bar and froze when I saw Jake standing there. Jillian was sitting next to me and I instantly gripped her arm.

"Ouch. What is that for?" she asked as she looked at me.

"What is Jake doing here? Did you tell him we were going to be here tonight?" I spoke through gritted teeth.

"Jake's here? Where?" She looked around.

"Answer my question!"

"No. I didn't tell him anything. It looks like he's with a group of people. I'm going to go say hi."

She got up from the couch before I had the chance to stop her. I sat and watched as she approached him and they began to talk. He glanced over and looked at me and I quickly turned away. A few moments later, Jillian walked over and sat down next to me.

"He's here celebrating his best friend Chandler's birthday with a group of people."

"Really? Of all the clubs in Los Angeles, he has to be at the one we're at?"

"So what? You created this awkward situation between the two of you, so deal with it. You work with him every day."

"Thanks a lot, Jillian." I gave her a dirty look.

"I'm going to dance. Want to come?" she asked.

"No. I'm staying here."

"Suit yourself." She shrugged as she grabbed Candace's hand and led her to the dance floor.

I grabbed my purse and headed to the restroom. After I finished washing my hands, I took my lip gloss out of my purse and began applying it.

"That's a great color," the woman with the long red wavy hair standing at the sink next to me spoke.

"Thank you."

"Would you mind if I looked at it?" she asked.

"No. Not at all." I handed it to her.

She turned it over and read the color on the bottom of the tube.

"Awesome. I think I'm going to get one for myself." She smiled as she handed it back to me.

"You should. I think it'll look good on you."

"Thanks. I think so too."

She placed her hand on my arm and I looked down at it and then back up at her.

"When one door closes, another opens, but your broken heart won't allow you to see what's meant to be and the open door that is right in front of you."

"Excuse me?" I frowned.

She reached in her purse, took out a card, and handed it to me.

"If you ever want to chat, you can call me or stop by my shop," she spoke as she walked out of the bathroom.

I looked at the card, which read: *Gemma James, psychic, spiritual healer, and owner of Gemma's Zen Shop* on Melrose Boulevard.

I shoved it in my purse and headed back to the table.

"Where were you?" Jillian asked. "I was getting worried. You didn't answer my text."

"I was in the bathroom. There was a long line. I'm sorry, but I didn't check my phone."

"I ordered you another cosmopolitan," she said as she handed me my drink. "The waitress is bringing out the cake for Candance in a minute and we're all going to sing 'Happy Birthday.'"

"Thanks."

A few moments later, one of the waitresses brought out a brightly lit cake with thirty candles stuck in it and we all started singing "Happy Birthday." Once we were finished and the waitress started cutting the cake for us, a look of horror swept over Jillian's face.

"What's wrong?" I asked.

"Well, well, look who it is," I heard Alex's voice from behind.

I froze as a sickness fell over me. I slowly turned around and faced him.

"Hello, baby," he spoke in a smug voice, and I cringed.

"What are you doing here, Alex?"

"A little birdie told me you'd be here tonight. You have my fifty grand you owe me for all my stuff you ruined?"

"Go to hell, asshole. You're not getting a dime."

"We'll see about that. Won't we?"

"Get the hell out of here, Alex. Nobody wants you here," Jillian chimed in.

"Jilly, is that any way to talk to your brother-in-law?" He held out his hands with a wide smile on his face.

"I never considered you part of my family." She stepped in between us. "Now leave or else I'll have security throw you out. This is a private party."

"Ha." He laughed. "This is a public place and I have every right to be here. Plus, I'm not going until Charlotte and I have a little talk."

He grabbed hold of my arm and I jerked myself out of his grip.

"Come on, baby, don't you want to talk? Isn't that what you promised we'd do when I got back to Seattle? But instead, I came home to all of my clothes in a pile of ashes and my most prized possessions shattered on the floor. You're still my wife, and if I say you're coming with me, you're coming." He grabbed my arm again and pulled me towards him. All I could smell was the whisky on his breath.

"I suggest you let go of her immediately." Jake walked up behind him.

"Get the fuck out of here, man. This doesn't concern you."

"The hell it doesn't concern me. Let her go, now!" he angrily spoke.

"Dude, I'm warning you."

"And I'm warning you."

"Jesus Christ, Charlotte. Do you know this clown?"

"Jake, it's okay. Please, just go," I begged.

"Ah. So you do know him," Alex spoke as his grip on my arm tightened.

"Ouch. Alex, you're hurting me." I tried to get out of his grip.

"You have two seconds to let go of her," Jake spoke through gritted teeth.

He looked Jake right in the eyes. "Are you sleeping with my wife?" Alex asked him as he let go of my arm, swung his, and planted his fist right into Jake's face.

I covered my mouth with my hands as Jillian grabbed me and pulled me back out of the crossfire. Jake returned the punch and sent Alex flying into the table. Alex got up and the two of them went at it. Everyone was watching, but nobody tried to break it up. Tears started streaming down my face as I begged them to stop. One more punch and Alex was on the ground. Jake bent down, grabbed him by his shirt, and raised his fist.

"Jake, don't!" I shouted.

He looked back at me and stared into my eyes.

"Who the fuck are you?" Alex asked.

"You want to know who I am? I'm the guy who saved your wife from being potentially raped at a bar back in Seattle the night she found out you were cheating on her. She was so drunk she didn't know what the hell was going on. Where were you? Her husband. The man who was supposed to protect her. That's right, you couldn't protect her because you're no man. You're nothing but a fucking coward. If I ever see you go near her or lay your hands on her again, I will kill you."

He let go of his shirt, stood up, and walked away.

24

Jake

I shook my fist to try and ease the pain as I walked out of the club.

"Jake, wait!" I heard Charlotte's voice from behind.

"Leave me alone, Charlotte."

She grabbed hold of my arm, so I stopped and turned around.

"You're bleeding. Let me help you."

"Go back inside. I really don't want your help."

"Bro, are you okay?" Chandler came running out of the club.

"I'm fine."

"You flattened that dude." He smiled.

"Happy birthday, bro. I'm going to head home."

"Yeah. Sure. I understand," he spoke. "Make sure to take care of that hand and put some ice on your face."

I looked at Charlotte as she stood there staring at me with her mascara-stained eyes.

"I'll see you Monday at the office," I spoke as I turned and headed to my car.

"I won't be there Monday, remember? I have my court hearing," she shouted.

I sighed as I climbed into my car and drove off.

When I got home, I packed a bag, headed to the boat, and set out into the open water for the next couple of days. I needed the alone time and I didn't want to be bothered by anyone.

ॐ

*C*harlotte
      I spent the entire weekend locked up in my apartment and mostly in bed. Jillian and my mom stopped by with some food, but I barely ate. I couldn't. I was sick to my stomach over the events of Friday night. Once again, Jake came to the rescue. He always seemed to be there at the precise time when trouble found its way to me. I was worried and I tried to call him a couple of times, but his phone went straight to voicemail. I didn't blame him one bit for the way he acted towards me since our talk on the beach. He confessed his love for me and I rejected him. If the circumstances had been different, I would have told him that I loved him back. I did what I had to do to save him from me, my fears, and my insecurities.

The next morning, my mom and Jillian came to pick me up to take me to the courthouse. I really wanted to go alone, but they insisted on coming and didn't give me a choice. I was exhausted and didn't want to deal with this, but then again, after today, I would be free of that bastard for the rest of my life.

"Everything is going to be okay, baby girl," my mom spoke.

I looked at her with a small smile and continued looking out the window of the car. When we arrived at the courthouse, Liam was waiting for me on the steps outside.

"Charlotte, good news. The judge who was hearing our case landed in the hospital over the weekend with a heart attack."

"Liam, that's awful news."

"Yes, of course. But good for us because the case was reassigned to Judge Mary Adams." He grinned. "She's a man-hating tyrant."

I took in a deep breath as we entered the courtroom and I saw Alex sitting on the other side. He looked at me with his swollen eye and bruised face and I couldn't help but let out a light laugh. I had just wished I was the one who put those bruises on his face.

"Oh dear. Jake did that?" my mother asked.

"He sure did." Jillian smiled. "It was awesome to stand there and watch that douchebag get the shit beat out of him."

"Remind me to thank that sweet man." My mother grinned.

I rolled my eyes as I took the seat next to Liam. A few moments later, Judge Adams entered the courtroom and we all stood up.

"Everyone can be seated," she spoke as she sat on the bench and picked up some papers. "In the matter of Foster vs. Foster, will both parties stand up."

Alex and I both stood. I could feel my knees shaking as my palms became sweaty.

"I had a chance to review all the documents presented in this case over the weekend due to the unfortunate incident with Judge Cornell. Let's tackle the divorce proceedings first." She glared at Alex for a moment. "What happened to your face, Mr. Foster?"

"It was nothing, your Honor. Just a misunderstanding."

"I see. Was your marriage a misunderstanding?" she asked and Liam glanced over at me with a smile.

"Excuse me, your Honor?"

"Your wife was the one who filed for divorce only after seven months of marriage."

"Yes," he spoke.

"And I see you've filed a civil suit suing her for fifty thousand dollars in damages to your personal belongings and emotional distress?"

"Yes."

"Why don't you tell me exactly what happened to your belongings?"

"I was in New York on business, and when I came back to our home in Seattle, I found she was gone and all of my clothes were in a pile of ashes in the backyard and some of my most valuable and prized possessions were smashed on the floor."

"That sounds to me like an act of a woman scorned," she spoke. "Any idea why she would do that?"

"Your Honor, everything is listed in the papers in the countersuit filed by Mrs. Foster. The fact is what she did was criminal mischief."

"I know that, Mr. Barnes. I don't appreciate you insulting my intelligence. Mrs. Foster, I want to hear from you why you destroyed your husband's clothing and other possessions." Her eyes turned to me.

"I was distraught because I found out he was cheating on me with a woman in New York. I wasn't in the right frame of mind and I apologize."

"Like hell you do!" Alex shouted.

"That's enough, Mr. Foster. One more outburst from you and I'll have you dismissed from my courtroom. It says here you have been together for ten years and married for seven months, correct?"

"Yes, your Honor," I spoke.

"Mr. Foster, did your wife ever display any kind of aggressive behavior or have any mental incapacities during the ten years you were together?"

"No, your Honor." He looked down.

"In regard to your divorce, I'm ruling it as an annulment. Mrs. Foster, as far as the courts are concerned, you were never married to this man. As for Mr. Foster's civil suit, I am awarding him the sum of fifty thousand dollars for the destruction of his personal property."

A sickness settled inside me as I placed my hand on Liam's arm.

"Yes! Thank you, your Honor."

"Don't get too excited yet, Mr. Foster. As for the countersuit that Mrs. Foster filed for emotional distress, which caused the act of temporary insanity because of the unfaithfulness of her husband, I am awarding her the sum of fifty thousand dollars. So, technically, you're not getting a dime, Mr. Foster. Move forward with your life and let this be a lesson learned. Next time you decide to get married, stay faithful and remember this day. Court is dismissed."

Liam turned and gave me a hug.

"I told you she was a man hater." He smiled.

I glanced over at Alex, who sat there with a scowl on his face, shaking his head.

As we walked out of the courtroom, my mom and Jillian hugged me tight.

"I told you everything would work out," Jillian spoke.

"Just for the record, Char, I did love you and I'm sorry," Alex spoke as he walked past me.

"Alex, wait!"

I walked over to him and stood there with tears in my eyes.

"Answer me one question before you leave. Why? Why did you throw ten years of our lives away?"

"I don't know. I really don't," he spoke and walked out of the courthouse.

25

---

*J*ake

The weekend I stayed on the boat, I decided I needed a vacation to get away from everything in California, including Charlotte, and clear my head. I booked a flight the next morning to Italy. The last time I was there was when I was seven years old. I didn't remember much, but what I did remember was enough to lead me there again. It was breathtakingly beautiful. I'd spent three weeks there studying the magnificent architecture and art, eating some of the world's best food and overlooking the Mediterranean as I nestled myself on the beaches in Venice. It was definitely a trip that should be shared with someone, but the alone time was what I needed. I met a woman named Nadia. She was attractive and we'd had a one-night stand. She was looking for some fun and I just wanted to forget about Charlotte. I felt guilty and I had no reason to. She didn't want to be with me, and she flat out told me that she didn't love me. But still, no matter how hard I tried, the guilt still resided inside me.

I had told my father everything that had happened that night and he understood why I needed to leave California. He approved my time off and took over the handling of the merger with Jillian for me.

But he made me promise that when I came back, my mind would be straight, and I would dive back into work full force without any distractions.

☙

I walked down the hallway with my briefcase in my hand and headed straight to my office.

"Welcome back, Jake." Natasha smiled. "How was Italy?"

"Thanks, Natasha. Italy was amazing." I smiled. "Can you grab me a cup of coffee and bring it to me in my dad's office? I'm heading there now. I'm still jetlagged."

"Of course." She grinned. "It's good to have you back."

I walked down to my dad's office and tapped on the door before opening it.

"Welcome home, son." He smiled as he walked over and gave me a hug.

"Thanks, Dad."

"How are you?"

"I'm good." I nodded my head. "It was a good three weeks to really clear my head."

"I'm glad to hear that. While you were gone, we secured a couple of new prospective clients. The files are on your desk."

"Here's your coffee, Jake," Natasha spoke as she walked into the office and handed me the cup.

"Thanks, Natasha. I better get back to my office, Dad. I have a lot of work to catch up on."

"Have you seen Charlotte yet?"

"No. I'm sure I will at some point today."

"And?" He cocked his head.

"Dad, I'm good. It was just bad timing for us. I've accepted it and moved on."

"Did you meet someone?"

"No. But when the time is right, I will."

I wasn't about to tell him about Nadia and the guilt that I felt. I took a seat behind my desk and opened the files that were lying in front of me. As I was looking them over, there was a knock on my door.

"What is it, Natasha?"

"It's not Natasha," Charlotte softly spoke as she poked her head into my office. "Hi."

"Hi."

I felt a twinge of pain in my heart as I stared at her.

"Did you need something?" I asked.

"Not really. I just wanted to welcome you back."

"Thanks. I appreciate that."

"How was Italy?" she asked.

"It was good, and a much-needed vacation."

"You left so suddenly."

"Yeah. I just needed to get away for a while. How is your work on the projects coming along?" I asked to change the subject.

"Good. I met with the clients and they're very happy. I had your dad sign off on the completed ones."

"Okay. Is there anything else? I really need to start looking over these files."

"No. That's it. I'll see you later," she spoke as she shut the door.

I leaned back in my chair and rubbed my forehead. Maybe three weeks in Italy wasn't enough.

harlotte
He hated me and I couldn't blame him. I didn't even know he went to Italy until I got back into the office on Tuesday when I went to tell him about my court hearing. I thought about him every day when he was gone and not seeing him around or talking to him for three weeks was extremely hard. I spent a lot of time trying to discover who exactly I was. As much as I didn't want to do anything at all except curl up in bed and stay there, I enrolled in a pottery class on Monday and Wednesday nights. Tuesday nights was Tai Chi.

Thursday nights was a cooking class and Saturdays were for goat yoga. Friday nights were reserved for curling up on the couch, eating takeout, and reading a self-help book. I kept as busy as possible to take my mind away from the chaos that was going on in my head, and for the first time in three weeks, the chaos quieted down the moment I saw Jake.

It was around lunch time when I got up from my desk and went into the break room to grab another cup of coffee. When I walked in, Jake was standing with the refrigerator door open grabbing a yogurt. He heard me walk in and turned around.

"Hey," he spoke as he shut the refrigerator door and went over to the drawer to grab a spoon.

"Hey." I nervously smiled. "Lunch?" I pointed to his yogurt.

"Pre-lunch snack. I'm meeting a client for lunch in about an hour," he said as he walked out.

26

ONE WEEK LATER

*C*harlotte
      Things were still the same with Jake. He barely looked at or spoke to me, only when he had no choice. When we did speak, it was very short and to the point. I was heading out of the building for lunch, reaching for my sunglasses in my purse, when a woman bumped into me and I dropped my purse on the cement.

"I'm so sorry," she spoke as she turned around and continued to scurry down the street.

"Thanks a lot!"

Looking up at the sky and letting out a long sigh, I bent down and started picking up the contents that fell out. This was getting old.

"Again?" Jake asked as he bent down, grabbed my wallet, and handed it to me.

"Thanks. Some woman just bumped into me and took off down the street."

Our fingers lightly brushed, and a feeling swept over me.

"I've got the rest. Thank you."

"Are you sure?"

"Yes. I know you have a lunch meeting." I gave him a small smile.

He returned the smile and I watched him as he headed to the

parking garage. The last thing lying on the cement was the card that woman gave me in the bathroom that night at the club. I picked it up and stared at it. The words she spoke to me that night still haunted me. I climbed into my car and sent Jake a text message.

"Hey, is it okay if I take the rest of the day off? I have something I need to do and I'm all caught up with work."

"That's fine."

"Thanks. I appreciate it."

I parked the car and walked into the shop. Looking around, I saw it was filled with everything from plants, books, crystals, tarot cards, oils, incense, etc.

"I've been waiting for you to come in," I heard a voice speak from behind.

When I turned around, Gemma was standing there with a smile on her face.

"Hi. To be honest, I don't even know why I'm here."

"Yes you do. You're seeking answers." She lightly placed her hand on my arm. "Come with me. Aubree, I have a client now, so keep an eye on the store."

"Sure thing, Gemma."

She walked me to the back of the store and into a small room that was decorated in different spiritual tapestries that hung on the wall with Buddha statues that sat in every corner of the room. Different plants filled the space and incense was burning.

"Have a seat." Gemma pointed to the small round table that sat in the middle of the room.

"You told me that night at the club that when one door closes, another opens, but my broken heart won't allow me to see what's meant to be and the open door that is right in front of me. What did you mean by that? And how did you know that I had a broken heart?"

She sat down with a deck of cards and gave me a smile.

"I just knew. I know a lot of things. Hold the cards in your hand and close to your heart for a moment," she spoke as she handed them to me.

I did as she asked, and she held out her hands and I placed the cards in them. She shuffled them and then laid them out in the shape of a pentagon.

"You've taken the lost path out of fear. You've been betrayed by someone you once loved and you've closed off your heart to the world. The man you were previously with was not the man you were supposed to be with, and if things didn't happen the way they did, you and your soulmate would never have met again."

"What do you mean?" I asked in confusion.

"Nothing happens to any of us without a reason or a purpose. Everything is divinely orchestrated."

"So you're saying that my ex-husband cheated on me for a reason?"

"Pretty much." She smiled. "Do you think it was a coincidence that your sister was in the right place at the exact time?"

"How do you know about my sister?"

"I have a gift, Charlotte. I was born with it. Both my father and my grandmother had the same thing." She flipped over four cards. "The door to your past is now fully closed, but you still feel a great deal of conflict."

"That's because I'm trying to find out exactly who I am."

"You already know who you are. You're using that as an excuse out of fear. The person you are resides in the soul of one man," she spoke as she flipped over two more cards. "Your soulmate and you've already met him."

I swallowed hard and she looked at me with a smile.

"The two of you were lovers in a past life. That's why the connection between you is so incredibly strong. You've found your way to each other again, but you won't let him in. That is what I meant when I told you that your broken heart won't allow you to see what's meant to be and the open door right in front of you."

"I'm not sure I believe in past lives," I spoke.

"You don't have to believe, but it's true. Two souls that were strongly connected in a past life usually find their way back to each other again. Think about how you felt when you first met. Did you have feelings you never felt before? Not even with the man you were married to? Does time stop when you're with him? Does the world around you fade away when you're together?"

Everything she asked was a yes answer, so I nodded my head.

"You didn't meet by accident. You met on purpose. All the events that happened to him and to you were leading up to the day you were reunited again."

"But the day we met was the worst day of my life."

"No, honey. It wasn't. It was the best day of your life." She smiled as she placed her hand on mine.

"Then tell me this. Why did I waste ten years of my life with a man I wasn't supposed to be with?"

"Only you can answer that. I'm afraid that's all I have for you. Change your direction, turn around, and don't be afraid. Your fear is interfering with destiny, and the perfect life you are seeking is right in front of you. Your souls are already entwined."

"Thank you, Gemma. How much do I owe you?"

"Nothing, Charlotte. This one is on me."

"Well, I can't let you do that."

I reached in my wallet, pulled out a hundred-dollar bill, and placed it on the table.

"Consider it a donation to your lovely store." I smiled.

I walked out, climbed into my car, gripped the steering wheel, and let out a deep breath. I felt like I had been punched in the chest, but at the same time, I felt free. Free of conflict, confusion and fear.

27

*C*harlotte

        I drove to the beach and sat in the sand by the shoreline as I listened to the whispers of the ocean. The things Gemma said hit me hard and caused me to sit and reflect on everything about Jake. Him being there on the sidewalk when I dropped my purse. Him being at the same bar as me that same night. Jillian being hired to be the corporate attorney for his company. Him being my boss and him being at the club that night to save me from the clutches of Alex. Nothing happened by accident. He was placed in my path every single time. Suddenly, I felt a warm sensation flow through me. I didn't know what it was, and I didn't know how to explain it. All I knew was that I had to go to Jake and tell him how much I loved him.

    I climbed in my car and drove to his house. He had to be home by now, and if he wasn't, I'd wait. His car was in the driveway and I let out a sigh of relief. When I walked up to the door and knocked on it, a woman with brown hair and green eyes stood there.

"Hi. Can I help you?"

A sickness settled in my belly as I stared at her.

"I'm sorry. I have the wrong house."

I turned around and headed back to my car, my heart pounding out of my chest.

"Charlotte?" I heard Jake's voice shout.

I placed my hand on the handle of my car door as he ran over to me.

"What are you doing here?"

"I'm sorry. I shouldn't have come," I spoke without looking at him. "You have company and you're busy. I'm sorry." I opened the car door.

He wrapped his fingers around my arm and he forced me to look at him.

"Melinda is my cousin. She flew in yesterday from Colorado and she's staying with my parents. I'm having her over for dinner to catch up."

Suddenly, the sickness inside me ceased.

"Did you need something?"

"I need to talk to you, but we can do it another time."

"No. Come inside. Please."

I followed him into the house and he walked over to Melinda and quietly said a few words to her.

"Melinda, I'd like you to meet, Charlotte. Charlotte, this is my cousin, Melinda."

"It's nice to meet you, Charlotte." She smiled as she extended her hand.

"It's nice to meet you too."

"Well, I'm going to head back to your parents' place. Thanks for dinner." She kissed his cheek.

As soon as she walked out and shut the door, Jake offered me a glass of wine.

"Yes, please. In fact, just give me the bottle." I took it from his hand.

He chuckled. "Why? What's going on?"

I swallowed the hard lump in my throat as I brought the bottle up to my lips and took a few sips.

"Charlotte, you're kind of freaking me out here."

"I love you, Jake Collins," I blurted out.

He stood there with his arms folded and his head cocked.

"You love me?"

"Yes." I took another large sip of wine. "Me and you," I paced around the room, "we didn't meet by accident. We met because we were supposed to meet. Your ex-girlfriend cheated on you because she was supposed to. Alex cheated on me because he was supposed to." I continued to pace back and forth. "You were meant to find me on that sidewalk and in that bar back in Seattle." I brought the bottle up to my lips. "Every meeting we had was planned by the universe because we were supposed to be reunited. We were lovers in a past life and we needed to find each other again."

Jake walked over to me with a smile on his face, took the bottle of wine from my hands, and set it down on the table. Then he placed his hands firmly on my shoulders to stop me from pacing.

"I love you, Charlotte." He grinned. "I never stopped loving you."

I relaxed my body and fell into his arms.

"I love you too and I always knew it. I was just so afraid of getting my heart broken again."

"I'll never break your heart. God, it feels so good to hold you again." His grip tightened around me. He broke our embrace, placed his hands on each side of my face, and softly brushed his lips against mine. "Past lovers?" His brow arched.

"Yes. That's why our connection to each other is so strong."

He pulled me into him and held my head against his chest.

"Then I hope we have many more lives together."

28

*J*ake

We were lying in bed, our bodies tangled in each other's after the fantastic sex we'd had. Her head softly rested on my chest as I struggled with the fact that I had to tell her about Italy. I didn't want any secrets between us.

"I need to tell you something," I fearfully spoke.

"What is it?" She lifted her head and looked at me.

I slowly closed my eyes and took in a deep breath.

"I had a one-night stand in Italy. It was only one time. It meant absolutely nothing, and I did it to try and forget about you."

She sat up, held the sheet against her body and stared at me with a sadness in her eyes.

"Thank you for being honest with me. We weren't together and I had told you that I didn't love you. I couldn't expect you not to sleep with someone else."

"You're not mad?"

"How could I be? We were barely friends at that point. Did it work?" The corners of her mouth slightly curved upwards.

"No." I brought my hand up to her cheek and softly stroked it.

"There isn't a single woman in this world that could ever make me forget about you. You're my soulmate, Charlotte Foster." I smiled.

ॐ

Two Months Later

*M*y and Charlotte's relationship was at an all-time high. Not only did we spend our days together, we also spent every night together, going back and forth between her place and mine. Life was good. In fact, it was perfect. My parents loved her and her family.

I stood in the bedroom while she was in the bathroom and pulled the diamond ring from my pocket. I just needed to figure out the perfect time and place to ask her to marry me. The moment I heard the bathroom door open, I placed the ring back inside my pocket. She walked over to me with her hand behind her back and brushed her lips against mine.

"I love those surprise kisses." I grinned.

"I have another surprise." She bit down on her bottom lip.

"What surprise is that, sweetheart?"

She took her hand from behind her back and held up what looked like a pregnancy test with the word "pregnant" lit up on it. My heart started to pound out of my chest as I stared at it.

"We're having a baby?" I asked in excitement.

"We're having a baby." She grinned.

I swallowed hard as I placed my hand in my pocket and pulled out the ring.

"Then I guess this is the perfect time to ask you to marry me."

She placed her right hand over her mouth as I held the ring up in front of her and got down on one knee, taking hold of her left hand.

"Charlotte, I love you so much and I never want to live without you. We were destined to be together and I want to love you and only you for the rest of my life. Will you marry me?"

"Yes, Jake! Yes. Yes. Yes. I will marry you." She beamed with excitement.

I placed the ring on her finger, stood up, and kissed her as hard as I could.

"I can't wait to tell our families," she spoke.

"Do you think they can handle both pieces of news at the same time?"

"We'll find out." The corners of her mouth curved upwards. "Let's tell them tonight. We can have a little dinner party."

"Good idea. You get on the phone with your family and I'll get on the phone with mine."

We parted ways and each called our families.

"My mom and dad are available for tonight," I spoke.

"So are my parents and Jillian and Chris."

"Excellent. Let's start planning." I kissed her lips. "We're having a baby." I pulled her into me and held her tight.

"And we're getting married," she said.

"Life is perfect, Char."

"I know it is and I'm so incredibly happy."

29

*C*harlotte

The next couple of months were crazy busy with planning a wedding on such short notice. I wanted to marry him and be able to fit into a dress before I started showing, which only gave us a couple of months. We had a small wedding, and as far as I was concerned, that was the only wedding I'd ever had.

We were married in a small ceremony on the beach and then had the reception at the Beverly Hills hotel, which consisted of about two hundred and fifty people. Then it was off to the Maldives, where we would spend an amazing two weeks for our honeymoon.

I put on my bikini and stared at myself in the mirror with my hands on my belly, which was already starting to protrude. Jake walked up behind me and placed his hands over mine.

"You're starting to show." He smiled.

"I know. It's like I popped out of nowhere."

"You're beautiful, Charlotte, and I can't wait to watch our baby grow every day."

"You know my ultrasound is scheduled the day after we get back. Do you want to know the sex?"

"If you do, I do."

"I just think it'll be easier to plan the nursery instead of decorating it gender neutral."

"I agree. I have something for you, and I've been waiting for the perfect time to give it to you, but I don't want you to feel overwhelmed."

"What is it?" I asked.

He walked over to where his suitcase sat and pulled out a large sheet of paper and spread it across the table in the living area of our suite.

"I bought this property for us prior to our wedding and I want us to design and build a home. It's just down the road from where the beach house is now."

"We have a home," I spoke.

"I know and I love it, but I want to build a new home. A home that we both designed and built together. We're newly married, we're having a baby, and we should have a new home. A home where we can make the most amazing memories in."

Tears filled my eyes as I stared at the paper.

"I love it and I love you." I reached up and brushed my lips against his.

"I love you too. So you like the idea?"

"I love the idea. Can we get started on it now?"

"God, I was hoping you'd ask me that." He wrapped his arms around me and swung me around.

He grabbed his laptop and we took it out onto the balcony that overlooked the ocean and got started on designing our home together, on our honeymoon without any distractions from anything or anyone. It was perfect, just like I'd always dreamed.

The day we got back from our honeymoon, his parents had a dinner party for us with my family to celebrate our return.

"Look at you. You've only been gone two weeks and you're already showing." My mother smiled as she hugged me.

"It's good to be back, Mom."

Jake opened his laptop and set it on the table in front of his father and called everyone over.

"Charlotte and I wanted you all to be the first to see this. We designed our new house and we're going to start building as soon as possible."

"You spent your honeymoon designing a house?" His dad's brow arched as he looked at him.

"We sure did, Dad, and it was great." He grinned.

"It's beautiful, son. The two of you did an outstanding job. But what's wrong with the house you already have?"

"Nothing, Dad. Nothing at all. I just wanted a house that we built together as husband and wife." He hooked his arm around me.

Six Months Later

"*How* are my girls?" Jake asked as he walked into the kitchen and kissed my belly and then my lips.

"We're fine." I smiled.

"I miss seeing you at the office." He wrapped his arms around me.

"I've only been on maternity leave for two days." I laughed.

"Two days too long as far as I'm concerned."

"Your mom stopped by today and helped me put the finishing touches on the nursery."

"She did? That's great. I know she's excited about the baby."

"Yeah. She is. There's something I need to talk to you about."

"What is it, sweetheart?" he asked as he opened the refrigerator.

"I already talked to your mom and of course she cried and gave me her blessing."

"About?" His eye narrowed at me.

"I want to name the baby Sadie."

"Are you serious?" he asked.

"Very serious, Jake." I smiled.

He shut the refrigerator door and wrapped his arms around me.
"You have no idea how much this means to me."
"Good. Then it's settled. We have a name for our baby." I grinned.
"I love you so much," he whispered in my ear as he held me tight.
"I love you too."

30

Jake

"Jake. Jake, wake up," Charlotte spoke.

"What is it?" I asked as I quickly sat up.

"My water broke. We need to go to the hospital."

"Oh my god. Okay. Stay calm."

I threw back the covers and climbed out of bed. Turning on the bedroom light, I grabbed some clothes from my closet.

"Stay calm, sweetheart. Everything is going to be okay," I quickly spoke.

"Jake, I am calm. You're the one who's freaking out," she said as she pulled on a pair of pants and a top.

"I'm not freaking out."

I grabbed the hospital bag off the chair.

"Are you ready?" I lightly grabbed hold of her arm.

She looked down at my feet and then back up at me.

"Are you going in your slippers?" She smiled.

"Shit. I think maybe I do need to calm down."

"Yeah. You do." She laughed.

I had no idea how she could remain so calm. I was excited but nervous at the same time. Her water breaking didn't seem to faze her at all. She remained as cool as a cucumber until the first contraction hit in the hospital. When it was over, she grabbed my shirt.

"Drugs. I want drugs now!"

"I don't think it's time yet, sweetheart."

"I don't care!" she screamed as another contraction hit.

After a few more contractions, she finally got her epidural and she was fully relaxed.

"I'm sorry I yelled at you," she spoke as she stroked my cheek.

"It's okay. I know you didn't mean it."

"Oh, I meant it. The pain was unbearable. I'm just sorry that I did it."

I smiled, leaned over, and kissed her lips. Both of our families visited until the time came that Charlotte had to push, and then they waited in the waiting room. After two hours of pushing, I heard my daughter cry as the doctor held her up.

"Congratulations, you two, you have a beautiful daughter."

Tears sprang to my eyes as I looked at her and the doctor handed me the scissors to cut the cord. Next to marrying Charlotte, this was the most beautiful time in my life. The nurse placed Sadie in Charlotte's arms as tears fell down her face as she stared at our daughter for the first time.

"She's perfect, Jake."

"She's perfectly you," I said as I kissed her forehead.

31

ONE YEAR LATER

Charlotte

Jake and I stood inside our almost completed six-thousand-square-foot new beach home.

"Just think, one more month and we'll be able to move in." He smiled.

"I can't wait. Everything looks perfect." I smiled as I walked around.

"Do you like your new home, Sadie? Daddy built a huge play-room for you." He walked her over to the French doors that led to the patio and showed her the large infinity pool. "See that?" He pointed. "You and Daddy are going to have so much fun swimming in the pool."

"And what about Mommy?" I raised my brow at him.

"Me and you are going to have our own fun in the pool." He winked before kissing my lips.

We walked upstairs and stepped into the room that was Sadie's. It was an exact replica of her room at the other house.

"Excuse me, Mrs. Collins?" Jerry, our painter spoke.

"Yes, Jerry?"

"You haven't told me what color you want this room painted?"

I stepped into the bedroom next to Sadie's and looked around.

"I'll let you know in a couple of months." I grinned.

"Congratulations."

"Thanks. Mr. Collins doesn't know yet."

"My lips are sealed." He walked out of the room just as Jake and Sadie walked in.

"You haven't decided on a color yet, sweetheart? It's the only room left in the house."

"I have a couple colors in mind."

I reached into my purse and grabbed two swatches and the tape. Walking over to the wall, I taped both colors up.

"It's either going to be pink or blue. I told Jerry we'd let him know in a couple of months." I smiled.

"Charlotte, are you?"

"Yes." I excitedly nodded my head. "I'm pregnant again."

I could see the tears fill his eyes as he walked over to me and hugged me tight.

"I can't believe we're having another baby."

"Are you happy?" I asked.

"The happiest man on Earth."

He broke our embrace and tenderly kissed my lips.

Six Months Later

We were settled in our new home and I was bigger this time around than I was with Sadie. I stepped into the nursery and stared at the light blue and gray walls and all the décor that was fit for a prince.

"It looks great in here," Jake said as he walked up behind me and placed his hands on my belly.

"It sure does. Where's Sadie?"

"I just put her down for the night. Swimming really wore her out.

I think we need to do that every day." He chuckled. "I need to go make a couple of calls. There was an offer on the other house."

"That's great. I'll be down in a minute."

He kissed the side of my head and walked out of the room. I opened the linen closet to put some sheets away, and I spotted a box that hadn't been unpacked yet. I took it out, and when I opened it, I saw my journal sitting on top. Removing it, I took it to the bedroom and sat down on the edge of the bed. Opening it up, I began to read it.

D ear Journal,

One day I'm going to meet the man of my dreams who will sweep me off my feet. We're going to get married, live in a huge beautiful home that I designed, and have two children that we'd spoil rotten. My husband is going to love me and only me because I am his world and his mere existence and he will never hurt me. Our souls will become one, never to be ripped apart. He is my soulmate and I love him with all of my heart.

I sat there and wondered if I wrote that because I had some sort of memory from a past life. Maybe? Who knew? Everything I wrote had come true and I was living my perfect life. A life I designed for myself when I was eight years old.

"Are you ready for bed?" Jake asked as he walked into the bedroom.

"Isn't it kind of early?"

"I didn't say we were going to sleep." He smirked.

I stood up and wrapped my arms around his neck.

"Then by all means, I'm ready." I softly kissed his lips.

ABOUT THE AUTHOR

Sandi Lynn is a *New York Times, USA Today* and *Wall Street Journal* bestselling author who spends all her days writing. She published her first novel, *Forever Black*, in February 2013 and hasn't stopped writing since. Her addictions are shopping, going to the gym, romance novels, coffee, chocolate, margaritas, and giving readers an escape to another world.

Be a part of my tribe and make sure to sign up for my newsletter so you don't miss a Sandi Lynn book again!

Facebook: www.facebook.com/Sandi.Lynn.Author
Twitter: www.twitter.com/SandilynnWriter
Website: www.authorsandilynn.com
Pinterest: www.pinterest.com/sandilynnWriter
Instagram: www.instagram.com/sandilynnauthor
Goodreads: http://bit.ly/2w6tN25
Newsletter: http://bit.ly/2Rzoz2L

Printed in Great Britain
by Amazon